It was the perfect Christmas tree.

She was in the woods with Griffin and his charge when they found it, and Joey couldn't stop extolling its merits. Griffin, though, was looking at her.

His breath tickled her ear when he said, "I don't know how I ever got through life without you."

"Don't say things like that," she admonished, even as her heart skipped a beat.

"It's the truth." He kissed her cheek, doing crazy things to her senses. "You're a miracle worker with Joey. He's actually happy."

She lifted a mittened hand to his cheek. "Because he has you."

How had she ever thought she could keep this man out of her life forever?

It had only been weeks since he'd become a guardian but he was different, grounded in a way she could have never imagined. It was deeply appealing, and she could almost feel her ovaries doing a happy dance. Oh, yes. Every part of Maggie appreciated the new and Improved Griffin Stone.

Every cell in her body wanted him.

And her recently patched-up heart loved him.

She was in trouble. Big-time.

* * *

The conclusion of Maggie & Griffin's trilogy!

Dear Reader,

I hope you love holiday stories as much as I do! *A Stonecreek Christmas Reunion* is the final installment in Maggie and Griffin's love story, and it was both exciting and emotional to wrap up their journey.

Maggie is trying to ignore her broken heart by focusing on the town and wooing a powerful new business to Stonecreek. When she realizes that Griffin had a good reason for walking away, she's tempted to give him another chance but still scared of opening her heart to him again.

Griffin has some wooing of his own in mind, namely winning Maggie back. He knows he's hurt her badly but comes to see that Stonecreek is truly his home, and Maggie will forever hold his heart. But it might be too late to make things right between them.

To me, there is no better time than the holidays to look for a little magic, and Maggie and Griffin are going to need a bit of their own to finally get their happily-ever-after. Thank you so much for joining me on this three-book adventure, and may your holidays be filled with love and magic!

You can always find me at www.michellemajor.com or connect with me on Facebook or Twitter.

Happy reading,

Michelle

A Stonecreek Christmas Reunion

Michelle Major

⬧HARLEQUIN®SPECIAL EDITION

Recycling programs
for this product may
not exist in your area.

ISBN-13: 978-1-335-46610-5

A Stonecreek Christmas Reunion

Copyright © 2018 by Michelle Major

Printed in U.S.A.

Michelle Major grew up in Ohio but dreamed of living in the mountains. Soon after graduating with a degree in journalism, she pointed her car west and settled in Colorado. Her life and house are filled with one great husband, two beautiful kids, a few furry pets and several well-behaved reptiles. She's grateful to have found her passion writing stories with happy endings. Michelle loves to hear from her readers at michellemajor.com.

Visit the Author Profile page
at Harlequin.com for more titles.

To the Special Edition readers—
thank you for inviting me into your reading lives.
It's a great honor.

Chapter One

"More lights."

Maggie Spencer surveyed the work taking place in the town square, a mix of confidence and anxiety spiraling through her. Her small town of Stonecreek, Oregon, was about to be thrust into the national spotlight.

Or at least the social media spotlight. LiveSoft, a wildly successful software and mobile app development company, was searching for a new location for its company headquarters. The over-the-top lifestyle in Los Angeles, their current location, clashed with the app's branding and corporate culture. LiveSoft was all about using technology to slow down and simplify life. LA wasn't a great place for that.

So in conjunction with a request for proposals, the company had launched a marketing campaign during which its social media followers would help determine which Pacific Northwest city would be the best fit for a company move.

As Stonecreek's recently reelected mayor, Maggie was determined to make sure her town was chosen and had been working around the clock since the election to that end. Stonecreek had arrived late to the proverbial party, finding out about the proposal deadline only a week before submissions were due. But she'd been thrilled to learn just before Thanksgiving that her town had been short-listed by the company's CEO.

And why not? Stonecreek was only an hour south of Portland and she liked to think the community boasted the potential workforce, opportunity for growth and work-life balance LiveSoft had outlined in their preferences. The company was best known for its mobile app that claimed to "balance internal life with the outer world." Of course, she had yet to download the app herself, but it was on her to-do list along with a million other items.

"We've already added two dozen extra strands." Jacob Snow, head of the town's maintenance department, had been coordinating the town's holiday decorations for the past two weeks. "At this rate you're going to be able to see this place from the moon."

"There's no such thing as too festive," Maggie told him.

"You ever seen that National Lampoon Christmas movie?" Jacob asked with a soft chuckle. "I feel like Clark Griswold out here."

Maggie frowned, looking around at all the activity with fresh eyes. The entire town square was draped with lights while a huge, elaborately decorated fir tree stood in the center of the park waiting for tonight's tree-lighting ceremony. An almost fifteen-foot tall menorah had been given pride of place in front of the main archway into the square, ready to be lit on each of Chanukah's eight nights. Wreaths had been draped over every lamppost and nearly life-size nutcrackers lined the main path. In addition to a makeshift stable that had been built to house the nativity-scene animals, there was a display of Santa riding his sleigh, complete with reindeer painted by the high school's art department, and all the planters situated through the park burst with oversize ornaments and colorful dreidels.

"Oh, my." She clasped a hand to her chest when her heart started beating out of control. "Is it too much? Our theme is winter wonderland. I don't want it to be gaudy. Are we trying too hard? It has to look effortless, like the holidays in a TV movie. Charming and quaint, not over-the-top. Should we take down some of the lights? What about the live manger? I knew those goats would cause trouble."

Jacob stared at her for several seconds then climbed down from the ladder. He'd been working for the town since Maggie was a girl, hired when her grandmother had been mayor.

He'd never married and rarely dated as far as Maggie knew. In fact, Jacob Snow was a bit of a mystery, keeping the town running smoothly but rarely participating in the myriad of festivals and fairs that delineated the seasons in Stonecreek throughout the year. Other than his silver-white hair, he looked very much like he had twenty years ago when Maggie first met him.

"Slow down. It will be beautiful," he said, awkwardly patting her shoulder like he knew she needed comfort but wasn't sure how to offer it. "Like it always is."

"This year is different," Maggie whispered. "It matters more."

"Because of that new company thinking of coming here?" He reached for another strand of lights.

She nodded. "LiveSoft is one of the fastest-growing technology companies in the region. It would mean new jobs and increased tax revenue for the town. We could fund programs for impacted kids in the school district. Some of those maintenance requests you've put in would be approved."

"Like a new snowplow?" he suggested with a wink.

"Exactly." She drew in a slow breath. "I'm freaking out."

Jacob smiled. "I hadn't noticed."

"There's no reason for me to freak out, right?"

"None at all."

"But there's so much I want to do for Stonecreek. Now that I'm mayor—"

"You've been the mayor for two years," he reminded her. "You were *re*elected by a landslide last month."

She sighed. "Yes, but it feels different now. I feel like the town elected me and not Vivian Spencer's granddaughter. It changes everything."

Maggie had finally stepped out from behind the long shadow her grandmother cast. The Spencers had been one of Stonecreek's most powerful families since the town was founded in the mid–eighteen hundreds. But Maggie's grandma had taken their leadership to a whole new level. As soon as Grammy married into the family, she'd made it her mission to ensure the Spencer name was synonymous with Stonecreek.

Grammy had been the biggest force in Maggie's life, especially after she'd stepped in to help when Maggie's mother died eleven years ago. Maggie owed Grammy so much—they all did—but she also wanted a chance to make her own mark on the town. She loved this community.

Although she'd won the election, the months leading up to it had been tumultuous to say the least. Her opponent had been Jason Stone, cousin of her ex-fiancé Trevor who she'd left at the altar last spring when she'd discovered he'd been cheating on her.

As if that didn't complicate things enough, she'd then fallen for Trevor's brother Griffin, the blacksheep of the Stone family, who'd returned to town to work on the vineyard the family owned and operated outside town. When Griffin broke her heart a little over a month ago, it had made her question everything.

Everything except her dedication to the town, which was why she had to do an amazing job as mayor. Her work was everything to her now. She might be a dismal failure at love, but she could succeed at this.

"Maybe you're the one who's changed," Jacob told her gently. "I've known you since you were a wee girl, Ms. Maggie. You were always the apple of your grandmother's eye. She wouldn't have encouraged you the way she did if she didn't think you could handle it. I see how hard you're working for the town. Everyone around here does, and we appreciate it."

"Thanks, Jacob." Emotion clogged Maggie's throat. "I'm going to go check on Dora Gianelli at the bakery. It's the first business we're spotlighting as part of the campaign. What says holidays more than hot chocolate and a Christmas cookie?"

"Cocktail weenies and a beer?" he suggested.

She nudged his arm, the tension in her shoulders relaxing as she grinned. "When are you going to come to Christmas with our family? There's plenty of room."

"Vivian likes to keep things private," he said, scrubbing a hand over his whiskered jaw.

"Grammy would love to have you join us," Maggie countered, even though she'd never discussed the matter with her grandmother.

"She never mentioned it to me."

Maggie rolled her eyes. "She gets busy around this time of year. I'm not going to force you, but keep it in mind, okay?"

"Okay," he agreed. "I've got one more string of lights to hang." He held up a hand when she opened her mouth to comment. "Trust me on this. One more strand will be the perfect amount."

She nodded. "I'll see you later tonight at the tree lighting."

"The whole town will be here to make you look good." He rubbed a hand over his jaw once more. "I may even shave for the occasion."

She leaned in and bussed him on the cheek. "I'm lucky to have you."

Maggie watched for another minute as he climbed the ladder, feeling marginally better that she could accomplish her goal. There was no reason LiveSoft wouldn't want to come to Stonecreek. Nestled in the heart of Central Oregon's Willamette Valley, the town had great restaurants, outdoor activities, a fantastic school system and tight-knit community.

Groaning softly, Maggie realized she was becoming a bit too obsessed with work when even her internal thoughts made her sound like a billboard for the town.

She turned to head across the town square toward the bakery only to find Griffin Stone blocking her path.

He looked as handsome as ever, the bright afternoon sunlight shining off his dark blond hair. He wore a flannel button-down, faded jeans and work boots. She couldn't see his green eyes because of the sunglasses perched on his nose, but the set of his jaw and the way his broad shoulders remained rigid told her this wasn't going to be an easy conversation.

Fine. Maggie wasn't in the mood for easy when it came to Griffin. She'd had plenty of time to get over him. She *was* over him so she could certainly manage a few words without losing her mind.

"I'm busy," she said and started down the path that would take her out the west gate of the town square. Stonecreek Sweets was on the north end, but she told herself she needed the exercise walking around the block would give her. Just because she *could* handle talking to Griffin didn't mean she wanted to handle it.

"You can't avoid me forever," came his rough reply from behind her.

"I can try," she said over her shoulder and quickened her pace. It didn't matter. Griffin caught up with her in a few long strides.

"Maggie, stop." He reached for her arm, but she yanked away.

"Do. Not. Touch. Me."

He held up his hands, palms out. "Fine. Okay. Sorry."

Her eyes narrowed.

"I'm so sorry," he whispered.

"It's fine," she lied.

"I called you." He ran a hand through his hair, looking past her. "Eventually."

She sniffed. "I blocked your number. Take a hint."

"This isn't you," he said, glancing back at her.

"Oh, yes," she shot back. "This is me. You know how I'm sure of that? Because I never left. I've been here the whole time. Some of us don't have the luxury to take off when things get too real, Griffin."

"That's not what happened. It's complica—"

"Don't say *complicated*. That word is off-limits with us," she told him. "Along with apologies. Remember?"

"I remember everything."

Despite her resolve to hate this man, his words felt like a caress against her skin, a secret promise and one she knew he could fulfill with remarkable skill. All the more reason to hold tight to her willpower.

"Go away," she said, not bothering to try to hide

the pain from her voice. Let him understand he hurt her. That was all on him.

He sighed. "Give me a chance to explain."

"I don't need an explanation. You ran off to your ex-girlfriend. Sends a pretty clear message, you know?"

"I called," he repeated.

"Almost two weeks after you left."

"Things were crazy and I—"

"You said you loved me," she blurted, and it felt like sandpaper coated her throat. "Here's some advice for next time. Don't say 'I love you' if it doesn't mean anything." She took a step closer to him, ignoring the tears that sprang to her eyes. So much for being unaffected. Maybe what she needed to truly move on was to get this out of her system. "If you love someone, you tell them everything. Not weeks later or when it's convenient. I don't know what happened between you and Cassie, and I don't care. Go to her again if that's what she needs. We're finished, Griffin."

"She died."

Maggie drew in a sharp breath and watched as Griffin pulled off his sunglasses and tucked them into his shirt pocket. His eyes were sad, almost hollow, and darn it all if she didn't want to reach out to him, offer whatever comfort she could.

But no. It was too late for that.

"I'm sorry," she said softly. "I know you loved her."

"I cared about her," he corrected. "I *love* you."

She shook her head. "Not in the way I needed you to."

There was the truth of it, and when he took a small step back like she'd hit him, she knew he felt the impact as much as she did.

He lifted a hand and used his thumb to wipe a stray tear from her cheek.

"Are you staying in Stonecreek?" she asked, because she had to know.

"I'm not sure yet." He cleared his throat. "There are extenuating circumstances."

She huffed out a humorless laugh. "I imagine one might even call them 'complications.'"

"One might," he conceded with a nod.

"Good luck with wherever life takes you." It was difficult to get the words out, but she even managed a small half smile to go with them.

"This can't be the end."

"We were naive to think it ever would have worked out between us."

He shook his head. "You know that's not true. Maggie, please."

"Please what, Griffin?" She threw up her hands. "What exactly do you want from me at this point?"

"I want another chance."

"No." She fisted her hands at her sides, her fingernails digging into the fleshy center of each palm until it hurt. Physical pain to mask another emotional hit. Of course, a part of her wanted to give in. It would be so easy. She could take one step forward and be in his arms again.

Except he was still holding back. She didn't know what it was or understand why, but she could almost see the barrier that surrounded him.

"I've got to go," she told him. "The tree lighting is tonight and it's a big deal this year."

"I heard about LiveSoft. I'm sure you'll put on quite a show for them."

"Yes, well…the show must go on and all of that. Goodbye, Griffin."

His jaw tightened. "I won't say goodbye," he whispered.

"That doesn't change me leaving," she said and walked away without looking back.

Griffin returned to the vineyard, his mood as black as a starless sky at midnight. He wasn't sure what he'd expected from Maggie. He thought he'd understood how mad she was, but other than that one moment when tears had filled her eyes, she'd been cold more than anything.

It had been like talking to some kind of vintage automaton, and the ice in her eyes when she looked at him made frustration curl along the base of his spine.

He kicked a piece of loose gravel in the driveway in front of his mother's house. The air was thick with the scent of wet earth from the rain that was so typical this time of year. He drew in a deep breath, hoping the earthy smells would ground him, as they always had in the past.

When he'd left home at eighteen after that final, awful fight with his father, Griffin had never expected to return. As much as he loved the vineyard, Dave Stone had made it clear that his oldest son would never be worthy of having any place in the family business.

Griffin still didn't understand the animosity that

had simmered between him and his dad back then. Yes, his mother had given him an explanation about his dad feeling trapped by her unexpected pregnancy and taking out his frustration on his older son. But Griffin couldn't imagine punishing a child for the things in life that didn't work out the way his dad wanted them to.

Especially now.

He'd been home only a day and had yet to talk to Marcus Sanchez, Harvest Vineyard's CEO, who'd announced plans to step away from his position right before Griffin left for Seattle. Griffin had no idea if Marcus still wanted him to take over the business, or if his abrupt departure had burned bridges with more than just Maggie.

As much as he wanted to get his former life back on track, he understood nothing would ever be the same. With another glance at the fields stretching out below the hillside, he headed for the house.

His mother, Jana, greeted him at the door, one finger lifted to her lips.

"Is he okay?" Griffin whispered, unfamiliar panic making the hair on his arms stand on end.

"Sleeping," she mouthed then motioned him into the house.

They walked through the foyer, and she stopped at the edge of the dining room.

Griffin's eyes widened as he took in the antique cherry table, covered with various blankets and sheets.

"In there?" he asked.

She gave him another strident finger to her mouth then led the way toward the back of the house and the big farmhouse kitchen that had been remodeled when he and his brother, Trevor, were in high school.

"I checked on him about ten minutes ago," she said, her delicate brows furrowing. "He was fast asleep, clutching that ratty blanket he carries everywhere."

"He calls the thing Chip," Griffin told her. "You never would have let Trevor and me cover the dining room table with blankets. As I remember, that room was strictly off-limits."

"I had to keep one room sacred from you heathens," she said with an equal mix of humor and affection. "Besides, neither you nor your brother dealt with anything near the trauma that boy has." She pulled a pitcher of iced tea from the refrigerator and glanced over her shoulder. "I heard him last night."

Griffin nodded, his gut tightening at the memory. "The nightmares are a regular thing since the funeral. He has to be exhausted."

"What are you going to do?" She poured two glasses of tea.

If he had a quarter for every time he'd asked himself the same question over the past few weeks...

When his ex-girlfriend and longtime friend, Cassie Barlow, had paid him a surprise visit in early October, she'd given no indication she was secretly interviewing him for the role of guardian for her four-year-old son, Joey. According to what she'd told him when he arrived in Seattle over a month ago, she hadn't known either.

Treatment for the breast cancer diagnosis she'd received over the summer had seemed straightforward, a course of chemo and radiation and she'd been don-

ning her own pink ribbon as a survivor. Then they'd
discovered the cancer had metastasized throughout
her body and within weeks, her prognosis had gone
from sunny to "put your affairs in order."

Being an eternal optimist, Cassie had still believed
she could beat the disease. It wasn't until hospice
intervened that she'd called Griffin. He'd arrived at
her bedside only to find out about her wishes for Joey.

The boy was polite and respectful but hadn't
warmed to Griffin at any point. Not that Griffin
blamed him. He'd tried to convince Cassie there must
be someone more appropriate for Joey than he was,
but she'd been adamant. He'd managed to have her
moved home with round-the-clock care at the end
and then spent four agonizing weeks sitting by her
bed and helping the nurses care for her before she'd
slipped away peacefully late one night. He'd hoped
the peace of her death might make things easier for
Joey.

Could anything lessen the pain and trauma of a
young child watching his mother die?

The night of the funeral had been the first time
Joey had woken screaming and thrashing in his bed.
The episode had taken years off Griffin's life, but
now he was used to the unsettling incidents. He'd
wake within seconds of hearing the boy and bound
to his bedside to comfort him. It was the only time
Joey allowed himself to be touched.

It made Griffin's heart break to feel that small
body trembling in his arms and damned if he had
any idea how to help the boy.

"I called Dr. Cunningham earlier," he told his
mother, massaging his hand against the back of his

neck. "To say he was surprised to hear from me would be the understatement of the year."

She smiled. "The thought of you calling your former pediatrician for advice is fairly shocking."

"I get it. He gave me the names of a couple of child psychologists to call. I'll try them on Monday morning. I think it would help if Joey had someone to talk to. I know it would help me."

"You're doing a good job," she said, placing a comforting hand on his arm.

"Only you could say that at this point." He laughed. "I've managed to muck up every part of my life once again. Maggie is done with me, and I can't imagine how Marcus took my absence."

Jana leaned one hip against the counter. "It would have helped if you'd let me talk to him about why you left."

Griffin shook his head. "I couldn't deal with people knowing when I wasn't sure what exactly was going to happen with Joey."

"Would you have stayed in Seattle if he'd put up a fight about coming here?"

"Of course. At least for a while. Hell, I almost wish he had resisted. Or showed any kind of emotion. It was like the sicker Cassie got, the more Joey retreated into his shell. I should have done more to bond with him, but I was so focused on her."

"She was lucky to have you," his mother told him.

"It's so unfair," he muttered. "She seemed happy and healthy when she came to visit in the fall. Maybe I'm not the right person to judge. Cassie and I were both a bit of a mess when we were together."

"Which is perhaps why the relationship didn't

work?" She sipped her tea. "You never talked much about her."

He shrugged. "We dated for six months when we were in our early twenties. To be honest, we were too much alike to be together in that way. I was drinking a lot and Cassie..." He closed his eyes as he remembered some of the wild times they'd had together. The memories were hazy and left him with a sick pit in his stomach. "Cassie had other vices. But she finally had her life on track, and she was a great mom."

"He's a sweet boy."

Panic tightened like a noose around Griffin's chest. "Am I going to screw him up, Mom? Should I have stayed in Seattle?"

"What do you think?" she asked softly.

"I don't know." He downed the glass of tea then set in on the counter, but the cool liquid did nothing to ease the burning in his chest. "Actually, I do know. He'll be better here, or at least I will, and that has to be better for him." He met his mother's gentle gaze. "I don't know how I could face this without you."

"I'm here for whatever you need."

Before Cassie's summons, Griffin had been staying in the efficiency apartment above the barn on the property. He'd planned to rent a place in town so that he and Maggie could have more privacy. Now he was back in his childhood bedroom, with Joey across the hall in Trevor's room. It had made the most sense logistically so that his mom could help with the boy.

"I want to be a part of Harvest," he told her. "This is my home. The grapes are in my blood."

"I know," she murmured.

"But Joey has to be my first priority."

"Yes," his mother agreed without hesitation.

"What does that mean for the CEO position?"

She lifted the pitcher and refilled his glass. "Your dad managed the company and his family. Being a father doesn't mean you can't run the vineyard as well if that's what you want."

"A father," Griffin repeated, a little stunned at the words.

"That's what you'll be to him. We're his family now."

Griffin nodded. Cassie had told him she didn't know who Joey's father was. She'd been an only child and her parents had died in a car crash when she was seventeen. She had no siblings and no relationship with any extended family.

"I need to talk to Trevor," he said, almost to himself.

"He's still angry at you for leaving." Jana's mouth pulled down at the corners. "At Marcus for wanting to wait for you to take over his job and at me for supporting him in that decision."

"Maybe Trevor has a point."

His mother shook her head. "He'll understand once you explain about Joey. I'm surprised the news didn't sway Maggie."

Griffin looked out the kitchen window. It overlooked the backyard, which included a large flagstone patio, built-in grill, seating area and a stone fire pit. Beyond that was an expansive yard with ornamental grasses and beds of perennials. It was the only part of the property they kept properly manicured.

He'd have to build a play set for Joey, as the one he and Trevor had used had been removed years ago. Maybe a tree house too. He'd always wanted one in the big maple tree in the corner, but his father never had time.

"I didn't mention it," he said, turning his back to his mom.

"Griffin." The word was a soft admonishment.

"I couldn't guilt her into taking me back."

"You hurt her badly."

"I get that." He felt a muscle tick in his jaw and pressed two fingers to it. "Maybe I didn't understand while I was in Seattle, but I do now."

"So you're going to let her go?"

He squeezed shut his eyes then opened them again. "What other choice do I have?"

"You could fight for her."

"What do I have to offer?" He lifted a hand, ticking off all the areas of his life that were in chaos. "I'm the guardian of a boy who just lost his only parent and will barely make eye contact with me. I have no actual job at the moment and I'm back to living with my mom."

"Maggie moved in with her father when she rented her house before the wedding."

"That's temporary."

"So is this," she reminded him. "You have a job if you want it, Griffin. You have a place at Harvest. You always have."

He laughed at the absurdity of that statement. "Not when Dad was alive."

"He would have come around eventually," his mother insisted.

"Doubtful."

"This isn't about your father. You love Maggie."

"Who knows if what I felt was even real. I'm not sure why I thought I'd be able to make a relationship like that work in the first place. My track record is spotty at best."

"You don't give yourself enough credit."

He stepped forward and drew his mom in for a quick hug. "You give me too much."

A faint sound drew his attention to the far side of the room. Joey stood in the doorway, clutching his blanket in one hand with his other thumb shoved in his mouth.

"Look who's awake," Jana murmured with a smile.

"Hey, buddy." Griffin plastered the biggest, brightest smile he could manage onto his face. "Did you have a nice nap?"

The boy shrugged.

"Would you like to make some cookies?" Griffin's mother asked. "I have ingredients for chocolate chip or peanut butter. Which do you like best?"

Joey stared at her for a moment then popped his thumb out of his mouth. "Peanut butter."

Jana let out what sounded to Griffin like a relieved sigh. She'd probably wondered if the boy would even answer her. "Peanut butter it is."

Joey stepped into the kitchen, the corner of his tattered blanket trailing across the travertine tiles. "Are you going to make cookies?" he asked Griffin.

"Um…" Griffin glanced at his mother then back to Joey. "I'd love to, but I need to do a walk-through of the vines before I meet with Marcus…" He paused, then clarified, "He's the man who runs the vineyard right now and I'm going to help with his job now that we're here to stay."

"I'm so glad to hear that," his mother whispered, squeezing his arm on the way to the pantry.

"I want to come with you," the boy mumbled.

Jana stilled.

"Are you sure?" Griffin scrubbed a hand across his jaw. "I'm just walking through fields, checking on rows of grapevines. Your... My... Ms. Jana here is offering an amazing afternoon filled with sugar and chocolate chips and—"

"I like it outside," Joey said simply.

Griffin glanced at his mother, who smiled and dabbed at the corner of her eye. "All those years when you'd try to follow your dad around while he worked. Who would have ever thought you'd be in his shoes?"

She meant the words as a compliment. A fond reminiscence of her late husband. Because of that, Griffin didn't correct her. But he wanted to. He wanted to shout and rail that he was nothing like his dad. If Joey wanted to shadow him in the fields, he'd let him and the afternoon wouldn't be filled with lectures and admonishments.

"Do you have boots?"

"Nope," came the boy's answer.

"Your gym shoes will suffice for now, but you'll need something sturdier as the weather gets colder."

"What's sur-fice?" the boy asked, his little brows furrowing.

"They'll be okay until we get you new shoes," Griffin clarified.

"Can the new ones have basketballs on them?"

"We'll see what we can do."

"Does that mean yes or no?"

Jana laughed then covered it with a cough. Griffin shot her a glare then returned his attention to Joey.

"It means I'll try," he told the boy.

Joey cocked his head, like a puppy studying his owner after being told to sit for the first time. The seconds ticked by, but Griffin didn't dare move. Somehow this moment felt like a test, and he'd never been great at tests.

"Okay," his new ward answered finally, and the tightness in Griffin's chest eased slightly.

Maybe trying really would be good enough.

"I'll have cookies waiting when you get back," his mom promised.

"Thanks," he told her and hoped she realized it was for so much more than just the promise of cookies.

His first instinct was to take Joey's hand, but he worried that would cause the boy to shut down. So he inclined his head toward the door. "Follow me and pay attention. Today is your first lesson as an apprentice vintner."

Joey fell into step a pace behind him. "What's a vintner?"

"Someone who makes wine."

"What's wine?"

Griffin shook his head as he led the way out the front door and started toward the hill that would take them down to the estate field, Inception, the first his father had planted. "It's grape juice for adults."

"I like chocolate milk," Joey reported.

"Of course you do." The boy had no idea what

he was talking about, but he was *talking*. The mere fact made Griffin smile for the first time in weeks.

With a little luck, he'd get his life back on track sooner than later.

Chapter Two

Maggie glanced around the illuminated town square later that night. Just as Jacob promised, everything looked perfect. She was relieved and grateful that so many residents had attended the lighting of the town Christmas tree and were now taking part in the Winter Wonderland festival. Sometimes it was hard to keep track of which event was happening on what night. Stonecreek's community calendar was as jam-packed as a socialite's in the middle of the Season.

But they were a small town without any big industry or corporation to anchor them. Tourism was a huge deal, all year round. The popularity of Harvest Vineyard helped with that, especially during the fall. That fact didn't make her breakup with Griffin any easier, just as it had complicated calling off the wedding to Trevor in the spring. Somehow she and their mother had managed to keep a friendly working relationship. Jana Stone had even become something of a mentor to Maggie, although they hadn't spoken much in the weeks since Griffin left for Seattle.

She hoped that could change now that he'd returned, whether or not he chose to stay. Maggie liked having an experienced woman to talk to and bounce ideas off since she was trying to pull back from discussing town business with her grandmother.

Grammy meant well but it was often difficult for her to remember that she'd retired from the position of mayor, and although Maggie loved her, she wouldn't be a puppet to her grandmother's whims regarding how the town should be run.

"Everything looks beautiful."

Maggie whirled around to find her grandmother standing directly behind her, Christian Milken, the CEO of LiveSoft, at her side.

Grammy frowned. "Mary Margaret, are you blushing?"

Maggie pressed a hand to her cheek and smiled at them both. "No, of course not. I think it's the cold."

"It's still nearly fifty degrees," her grandmother pointed out. "Unseasonably warm for December."

"I'm wearing a coat," Maggie said, even though the light jacket she'd worn over her red fit-and-flare dress offered little warmth, as it was more for fashion than function. She shrugged out of it anyway.

"That's a lovely dress," Christian said.

"Thanks."

"I'm curious to know what you were thinking of just then." Grammy shook her head and lowered her voice to a whisper. "No time to sit on your laurels, girly. We started off the competition with a bang but we'll need to keep up the full-court press if we're going to convince LiveSoft to choose Stonecreek."

"Right." Maggie offered an awkward smile to Christian. Even Grammy's quiet voice had a way of carrying. Now she really was blushing, embarrassed that her grandmother had so quickly and carelessly reduced an evening of holiday cheer to something almost mercenary in nature.

Yes, she wanted to win the competition—her town could use the influx of revenue and jobs. What town couldn't?

But tonight was also about having fun and kicking off the holiday season. Maggie loved Christmas. Some of her fondest memories from childhood, before her mother's death, were of how special the holidays had been. They'd cut down a real tree out in the woods every year, strung popcorn as garland and sung carols around the fire. Her mom had been a fantastic baker, and Maggie had been so proud to deliver cookies to neighbors and friends.

She'd tried her best to keep some of the family traditions alive once her mom died, but it hadn't been easy. Then she'd gotten busy with her own life and it felt like her family had lost something precious. She'd moved back to her house two weeks ago when the tenants she'd rented it to had decided to return to Alabama a few months early. But she'd vowed to make this Christmas extra special for her younger siblings, Morgan and Ben, and their father. Along with her extra work on the town's campaign for

LiveSoft, she hoped to keep herself so busy she wouldn't have any time to miss Griffin.

"I need to talk to Dora about the uneven icing on her cookies," Grammy said, already looking past Maggie. "Mary Margaret, entertain Christian please." Without waiting for an answer, Vivian walked away, much like Maggie imagined the queen would after giving an order to one of her faithful servants.

"I used to know how to juggle," she told Christian with a shrug. "But I'm pretty rusty and fresh out of props."

"Know any magic tricks?" he asked, raising a thick brow. "Or a good knock-knock joke?"

Maggie laughed and shook her head. "Unfortunately, no. But I do know the ladies over at the high school boosters' booth make the best hot chocolate in town. Would you like to join me for a cup?"

"That sounds perfect."

She glanced at Christian out of the corner of her eye as they got in line at the booth. He was handsome in a country-club sort of way, short blond hair and piercing blue eyes. He was always clean-shaven from what she'd seen and favored tailored shirts and pressed jeans with expensive-looking loafers.

She'd done her research on the CEO, born and raised in Boston to a former senator and his homemaker wife. Christian had attended private schools and then graduated from Harvard before moving to the West Coast to start LiveSoft. He'd been one of the company's founders, although she remained fuzzy on his role in developing the app. However, he'd become the face of the brand and was thought to be responsible for much of the company's meteoric growth.

In fact, social media and marketing were his specialties. The public campaign to help choose the company headquarters had been his idea.

"I hope you enjoyed tonight," she said, inclining her head toward the towering Christmas tree in the center of the square. "And not just because of the competition, despite what Grammy would have you think."

"It was great," he said. "Very Norman Rockwell."

"We're all community spirit around here," she said, then cringed. "I hate that everything I say to you sounds like I'm selling Stonecreek."

"I don't mind," he insisted. "We were in Timmins last night and they tried to manufacture snow and ended up causing a minor flood in the elementary school gym."

"Oh, my," she breathed. They stopped at the back of the long line for hot chocolate. "At least we didn't go that over the top." She arched a brow. "Unless you like over-the-top and I'll make sure to ramp things up."

"Move aside, people!"

Maggie glanced sharply toward the covered booth in front of them as the crowd parted. Grady Wilson, who ran the only locally owned gas station in town, made his way forward, elbowing people out of the way as he did. Grady's grandson was the quarterback for the high school football team, so he and his wife were very involved in the boosters.

Grady grinned at Maggie. "Our beloved mayor and potential beloved town savior shouldn't have to wait for a hot drink."

"It's fine," Christian called, waving a hand. "I don't mind waiting my turn."

"Town savior?" Maggie muttered, shaking her head. "I guess we've got over-the-top covered after all."

Grady approached them with a wide smile, a steaming cup in each hand. "Nonsense," he insisted. "I gave you both extra whipped cream too. Our Maggie here's a big fan of whipped cream."

Christian raised a brow in her direction, a small smile playing at the corner of his mouth.

She felt color rise to her cheeks again. Grady certainly didn't mean his comment to sound like a sexual innuendo, but somehow it came out that way.

As she thanked him for the hot chocolate, she noticed the assistant who'd filmed the lighting of the town tree earlier standing a few feet to the side, her phone held aloft like she was taking a video of this episode.

"You stick with Maggie," Grady told Christian. "She'll make sure you're in good hands."

Maggie darted another look at the camera then forced a bright smile. "Everyone in Stonecreek is excited about this opportunity," she announced. "Aren't we, folks?"

The people in line gave an enthusiastic round of applause—bless them—and Christian toasted Maggie's cup of hot chocolate. "To new opportunities," he said, making his voice loud enough to carry and earning more clapping.

As they turned to head back toward the center of the square, he leaned in closer. "And to extra whipped cream," he whispered, his voice teasing.

"That did not mean what you might have thought it meant," she said, looking over her shoulder. "Are we still on camera?"

He shrugged but kept his gaze forward. "Danielle was going to get some extra footage in case she needed filler, but I doubt it will be used and there's no audio with it."

"Okay, good. I'm not used to my every move being documented."

"Aren't you on social media?" he asked, brows pinching.

"Yes, but I'm not active. It doesn't come naturally to me."

"That's why you need LiveSoft," he told her. "The app can organize everything for you in a way that makes it less overwhelming and more streamlined." He pressed the heel of his palm to his forehead. "Now I sound like a walking advertisement for my own company. Sorry."

"No need to apologize. You have a great product. I do plan to use the app, although I'm horrible with technology."

"I could give you a tutorial," he offered. "Maybe over dinner one night next week? I'm heading out early tomorrow to get ready for a meeting on Monday, but I'll be back by the end of the week."

"Dinner?" she said, her voice coming out in a squeak.

"You've heard of it, right?" His smile was teasing and more than a little flirty.

Christian Milken was flirting with her. She fought the urge to check on the camera again. How was it possible that she'd just sworn off men, and suddenly, in the span of twenty-four hours, Griffin had reappeared and Christian was asking her out? Okay, wait. Maybe she was reading too much into this. If Stonecreek was chosen as LiveSoft's headquarters, he'd be relocating here. He probably was just being friendly…neighborly even.

"Of course," she said with forced cheer. "Dinner would be lovely."

"Not as lovely as you," he murmured and lifted his hand to trace a finger along her jaw.

So much for being neighborly.

A throat cleared behind Maggie, and she whirled around to find Griffin standing there, a wine bottle in each hand. His expression was dark as midnight, his green eyes intense on her.

"I hope I'm not interrupting," he said through clenched teeth.

She shook her head, swallowing down the lump of emotion that welled in her throat at the sight of him.

"Have you met Christian Milken?" she asked stepping back to include the CEO in the conversation.

"That's why I'm here." Griffin's voice was tight but he gave Christian a friendly smile. "I'm Griffin Stone from Harvest Vineyard. We donated a few bottles of wine for the silent auction earlier, and I thought you might like to add a couple to your collection."

Christian took one of the bottles Griffin held out and studied the label. "Pinot Noir. That's my preferred type."

"I heard." Griffin flicked a glance toward Maggie then back to Christian. "We're all excited about the potential of having you make Stonecreek your new headquarters. I can tell you it's a fantastic place for a growing business. The town does its best to make sure the business community is taken care of."

Maggie's fingers tightened around her cup of hot chocolate. Here was one more example of a perfectly innocuous comment sounding vaguely suggestive to her ears. Like she was personally responsible for servicing local business owners. She knew Griffin didn't mean it that way, any more than Grady had, and hoped Christian understood it too.

"I'm coming to appreciate what Stonecreek has to offer more with each moment," Christian said, inclining his head toward her.

Griffin's broad shoulders went even stiffer, if that was possible. Not that Christian would notice. Griffin wore faded jeans, another thick flannel shirt and a baseball cap with the Harvest Vineyard logo stitched on the front. To the casual observer, he'd appear to be relaxed and easy-going, just another resident helping to make a good impression.

But Maggie could feel the tension radiating from him.

"The business owners around here support each other," she said with patently fake cheer. "It's one of the things that make us stand out."

"Among others," Christian murmured softly.

"Harvest is a great example of that," she continued as if he hadn't spoken. "Griffin's father founded the vineyard. From the start, and especially in the past few years, they've become a leader in the Oregon wine industry."

Christian adjusted the scarf wound around his

neck and nodded. "I met your brother last week," he told Griffin. "He has some big plans for expansion."

"Yes, he does," Griffin agreed almost reluctantly. "But we're also focused on environmental steward-ship and the type of community we create. Our entire team contributes to the end product. We want to make our company healthy for the land and the people who work for us."

"I like the sound of that." Christian's blue eyes lit with interest. "Work-life balance is one of the tenets LiveSoft was founded on."

Maggie drew in a steadying breath as the two men discussed company culture as well as environmental building practices. She also had a moment to observe the two of them, both attractive but so different in looks and temperament. Despite his obvious enthusiasm for the topics, Christian remained almost aloof as he spoke with Griffin, every inch the tall and lean corporate executive. Griffin was earthy and raw, gesturing with his hands, his brows furrowing as he considered the other man's ideas. And when he scrubbed a hand over the stubble that shadowed his strong jaw, Maggie's insides tightened.

Would she ever not have that kind of visceral re-action to him?

"I'd like to set up a time to visit your operation," Christian said. "I was only planning on staying in town for a day next week, long enough to shoot foot-age for the next installment of the social media story. But if you could carve out an afternoon, I can push the next stop on my small-town tour?"

"Sure," Griffin said, glancing at Maggie. "Happy to show you around. Anything for Stonecreek."

She knew he wasn't happy to spend any more time with LiveSoft's polished CEO than was absolutely necessary. The look he shot her was brief, a slight raise of his brows and a flash in his green eyes. In that moment she understood the only reason he was being the least bit cordial was to help her.

What was she supposed to make of that after she'd just cut him out of her life a day earlier?

"Thank you," she told him.

"You should come out too, Maggie May," he answered with a far too innocent smile. "Our plans at Harvest might interest you, as well."

She opened her mouth to argue but Christian put a hand on her back. "Great idea. We can talk more about how LiveSoft might fit into the current community and what our employees are looking for with regard to the balance between work and their personal lives."

"Sure," she answered, her cheeks aching from so much fake smiling. "Um…text me."

"I will." Both men answered at the same time, only adding to the awkwardness of the moment, at least for Maggie.

She turned up the wattage on her smile, surprised her cheeks didn't begin to crack. "Sounds good," she answered both of them at once. "Right now I'm going to go help with cleanup."

"Doesn't Jacob Snow usually handle that?" Griffin asked.

"I'm here to support *everyone*," she said sweetly. "You fellas have a great evening." Without waiting for a response from either of them, she turned and walked away.

After tossing her empty hot chocolate cup into a nearby trash can, she massaged her fingers against her temples. Was it possible she'd sworn off men only to find herself torn between two of them?

Griffin stalked into O'Malley's Tavern after finally ditching Christian Milken. The man might run one of the hottest app-development companies in the industry, but he seemed like a total tool to Griffin. His distaste had plenty to do with Milken's obvious infatuation with Maggie.

Griffin had come to the Winter Wonderland festival under the pretense of checking on the Harvest wine donation, but he'd also hoped to see Maggie. His life might be an unholy mess at the moment, but he wasn't ready to give up on her. He understood the way he'd left had hurt her, and he wasn't ready to talk to her about Joey, but he'd returned to Stonecreek and planned to stay. Now he just needed Maggie to let him back into her life.

Granted, she wasn't aware of either of those revelations yet. In fact, Griffin had just made the commitment to himself earlier in the day. It was walking the fields with Joey that had done it. The boy had been fascinated by the rows of vines, reaching out to touch the curving stalks and listening intently as Griffin explained the growing cycle of the grapes. As his mother noted, the boy's interest had reminded Griffin of himself when he was a kid. No matter what had been going on in his life and how bad things had gotten with his dad, he'd always found solace in the fields.

He understood that Joey's grief from the loss of his

mother couldn't be easily overcome, but he believed with his whole heart that being in Stonecreek would be a help rather than a hindrance to the boy's healing.

As it had become for Griffin.

Maggie and her unfailing dedication to the community were a big part of what had helped him feel connected to the town again. She had every right not to trust him, but he was bound and determined to convince her he deserved another chance. He'd be the kind of man who deserved her.

Even if that meant helping to convince that far-too-slick-for-Griffin's-taste CEO to relocate his company there.

After just a few minutes in the guy's presence, Griffin needed a beer. He'd texted his mom and she'd confirmed Joey was sound asleep. One quick drink before heading back couldn't hurt.

He waved to Chuck, the bartender and longtime owner of the pub then slid onto one of the wooden stools in front of the bar.

"Fancy meeting you here," a familiar voice said, and Griffin suppressed a groan as he turned to see his brother, Trevor, in one of the booths that ran along the wall next to the bar.

"I called you earlier," Griffin answered, slapping down a crisp bill on the bar when Chuck placed a beer in front of him.

"You two plan to meet up like this?" the bar owner asked with a knowing wink.

"Lucky coincidence," Griffin muttered.

So much for a few minutes to unwind. He picked up the beer and moved to the booth, slipping in across from Trevor.

"To Christmas in Stonecreek," his brother said, raising a glass of amber liquid for a toast.

"I thought you only drank wine," Griffin told him.

"I'm making an exception for the holidays." He lifted his glass and drained it. "One more, barkeep," he shouted.

"Fine," Chuck called back. "But I'm cutting you off after that."

"I can walk home from here," Trevor protested.

"Understood, but your mom will kill me if you end up sleeping on the sidewalk. I'm not convinced you won't pass out on the way home."

"I'll make sure he gets there safely," Griffin said, looking back toward the bar owner.

Trevor gave a loud chuckle. "That's right. My big brother has my back. Ask anyone." His bleary gaze settled on Griffin. "Like Maggie."

"I thought we were past that." Griffin adjusted his ball cap then took a long drink of beer.

"Me too." Trevor shrugged. "You left again, and it hurt her."

"That's my problem," Griffin said through clenched teeth.

"It's not right," Trevor continued as if Griffin hadn't spoken. "You get to come and go whenever the mood suits you."

"It wasn't like that. Not this time or when I left years ago. You know that."

"Do I?" Trevor flashed a grateful smile at the waitress who set his drink on the table. "Thanks, sweetheart."

"I'm off in an hour," the young blonde told him

with a subtle wink. "If you need an escort home, I'm happy to oblige."

"Much appreciated," Trevor told her. "But this night is all about brotherly love."

The woman made a face.

"Not that kind of love," Griffin clarified. "He's too drunk to make any sense."

"I make perfect sense," Trevor countered. "You just don't want to hear the truth." He leaned forward across the table. "You can't handle the truth," he said, doing a really pathetic Jack Nicholson impression.

The waitress laughed then turned away.

"What the hell is going on with you?" Griffin demanded. "You never drink like this."

"I got offered a job today," Trevor blurted then sucked in a breath. He lifted the glass then set it down again. "I turned it down."

"What kind of job?"

"Marketing director for Calico Winery."

Griffin whistled softly. "That's huge, Trev. Calico is the biggest and the best when it comes to Sonoma vineyards."

"Don't remind me," his brother whispered.

"You didn't even consider taking the job?"

"How could I when I'm going to have so much fun working for you?" Trevor held out his hands. "You can take off for over a decade, show up for a few months then disappear again and still…" He pointed an angry finger at Griffin. "Still Mom and Marcus want you to take the helm. I've been here toiling away, trying to make a name for Harvest and no one even gives a rip."

"That's not true."

"I have plans for the vineyard," Trevor continued. "Plans to make us the biggest organic-certified producer in the Oregon wine industry. All I get is pushback for any idea I bring forward."

Griffin dragged a hand along his jaw, unsure of the best way to have this conversation with his brother, especially in Trevor's current state. They'd never been exactly close, not with their father's affection and approval so clearly favoring Trevor.

Dave Stone hadn't done either of his boys any favors with his preferential treatment of his younger son. Instead, he'd subtly pitted one brother against the other. Griffin had loved the vines, but Trevor had been the company's heir apparent.

Now that things were changing, Griffin understood it was a difficult pill to swallow. He also appreciated Trevor's dilemma. As angry as Griffin had been when his dad had all but kicked him out of their lives, it ultimately had been something of a blessing. He'd had a few years to make his own way in the world. He'd joined the army and then worked in construction around much of the Pacific Northwest. When he finally made his way back to Stonecreek, despite his varying emotions about this place, he knew in his heart the choice to stay would be his.

Trevor never had that choice.

"Maybe your plans are bigger than what Harvest can hold," he suggested quietly.

"Because you want to get rid of me?" Trevor's lip curled into an angry sneer.

"Because I want you to be happy."

Trevor's head snapped back like Griffin had punched him. "Why do you think Dad acted the way he did with the two of us?" he asked after a long moment.

Griffin sighed. He'd only recently learned the whole truth around the start of their parents' marriage. "Mom got pregnant with me to trap him into marrying her." It pained him to say the words, both because of the shadow it cast over his mother's character and what it said about how wanted he'd been as a baby. Which was not very much, at least by his dad.

"But he loved her," Trevor said, shaking his head and looking suddenly far more sober than he had a few minutes earlier. "Why would it matter how things started? And you had nothing to do with any of that."

"I don't quite understand it," Griffin admitted, "and Dad isn't saying much from beyond the grave."

"Damn, Grif," Trevor muttered.

"It wasn't easy for Mom to share it with me." He took another drink of beer then laughed. "Although it was better than the explanation I'd come up with on my own, which basically boiled down to questioning whether Dad was my real father."

Trevor made a face. "You look like Mom, but you're a chip off the old paternal personality block."

"Maybe, but I'd had fantasies as a kid of some Clint Eastwood–type guy showing up and claiming me as his own." He shrugged. "I could imagine every moment up until the point where I had to leave Harvest. Then it got fuzzy."

"You left anyway."

"Dad and I would have torn each other apart if I'd stayed." He blew out a long breath. "I'm sorry you felt like you didn't have a choice in the path your life took, Trev."

His brother massaged two fingers against his forehead. "It seemed like one rebel in the family was enough."

"You *do* have a choice." Griffin sat up straighter. "I'm not trying to push you out. If you want to stay at Harvest, we'll find a way to run the business together. But Calico might be a once-in-a-lifetime opportunity. No one would blame you for wanting to do something for yourself at this point."

"You want to check with Mom before you start making promises?"

"I don't need to," Griffin insisted. "She's not like Dad. You know that. She wants you to be happy, no matter how that looks or where it takes you."

Trevor leaned back, crossed his arms over his chest. "I always figured the family business was my only option. Dad made it clear—"

"He's gone," Griffin interrupted then shook his head. "The old man did a number on both of us, but I have to believe he meant well in his own narcissistic way. You can't let everything that came before dictate what comes next for you. You have big ideas and you're damn good at what you do."

"I love it," Trevor said softly. He looked down at the drink in front of him then added, "But I want more. I want to take the job."

Griffin nodded. "We'll talk to Mom in the morning, explain what's going to happen. She'll understand. We'll make sure of it."

"Thank you." Trevor's gaze lifted to Griffin's and there was a mix of anticipation and relief in that familiar gaze that made Griffin's chest ache. Why hadn't they talked like this before now? They'd lost so many years… Griffin had wasted so much time on anger and resentment. He hated himself for it, but all he could do now was vow to change.

"You ready to head home?"

Trevor rolled his eyes. "I'm not going to end up passed out on the sidewalk."

"Let me walk with you anyway. I have some big brothering to catch up on."

"Fine," Trevor grumbled but he didn't seem upset by Griffin's insistence. "I'm holding you to the offer to be there when I talk to Mom. She's going to freak out."

Griffin thought about their mother's calm reaction when he brought Joey home with him. "I think she'll handle it okay," he told Trevor with a smile.

They each climbed out of the booth, waved to Chuck and headed out into the cold December night.

Chapter Three

Jana opened the front door the following morning and felt her jaw go slack. Instead of her younger son, who Griffin had told her would be stopping to discuss something with both of them, Jim Spencer stood on the other side.

Her hand automatically lifted to smooth the hair away from her face. She wore no makeup and was afraid she looked every day of her fifty years. Joey'd had another nightmare at three in the morning. She and Griffin had spent over an hour trying to get him back to sleep, resulting in very little rest for Jana after that.

She stepped onto the porch and closed the door behind her. Griffin was working in the office that had been her late husband's, a room off the kitchen, while Joey remained asleep. Although she didn't approve of Griffin keeping Joey a secret from Maggie, she respected that the decision was his. Obviously, he wouldn't want Maggie's father discovering the boy before he was ready to share the news himself.

"What are you doing here?" she demanded, her tone harsher than she meant it to be.

Jim frowned, inclining his head to study her. He'd always had a contemplative air about him, the soul of an artist even before he became the renowned sculptor he was today.

"Are you okay, Jana?" he asked softly, reaching out a finger to gently trace the frown line between her eyes. A fat lot of good that would do. One of her friends had recently suggested a dermatologist in Portland who was known to be an expert with Botox. Jana had smiled and said she liked that her face told a story. Now she wished she'd called for an appointment.

"Fine," she answered, shifting away from his touch, which still elicited a tingling along her spine, much as it had when they'd been teenagers. Only she was nowhere near the naive girl she'd once been. "Griffin is on a call," she lied, "so he needs quiet."

Jim nodded, although the excuse was lame even to her ears. The old farmhouse was plenty big to accommodate the two of them without disturbing her son.

"We'd scheduled a meeting to discuss your commission," he said, holding up a slim file folder. "I did initial sketches and pulled some ideas into a file for you to review."

Right. The commission for a sculpture she'd discussed with him at the hospital fund-raiser she'd chaired over a month ago. What had she been thinking?

That she wanted something for herself.

That she wanted to feel alive again.

That she wanted another chance with the man who'd broken her heart over three decades earlier.

Jana kept her features placid even as panic and embarrassment washed over her in equal measure. She'd like to blame her impulsive request that he create a sculpture for the vineyard on the emotional highs and lows of menopause. What else could explain reaching out to Jim?

She'd moved on from her first lost love. For heaven sakes, they'd lived in the same town for years and she hadn't revisited her feelings.

"I'm sorry," she said coolly. "I know we agreed to meet after the Thanksgiving holiday, but I've been busy." She licked her dry lips. "Griffin had a rough time while he was away."

Jim's gentle eyes hardened as he shook his head. "I can't bring myself to have any sympathy for him. Not after what he did to Maggie."

"I know he feels terrible for hurting her."

"He's a scumbag."

"Jim."

"You'd think the same if our positions were reversed."

"Like when Maggie walked out on Trevor minutes before the wedding?"

One thick eyebrow lifted. "Because she discovered he was cheating on her. I hardly think it's the same thing."

She shook her head. "I hate that my sons have hurt your daughter."

"I'm afraid Maggie is somehow paying the karmic price for how I hurt you once upon a time."

"That isn't how karma works," she whispered, not trusting her voice to manage anything steadier. It was the first time he'd acknowledged the pain he'd caused. "We both moved on a long time ago, made our own lives."

He turned, looked out toward the view of the fields below. She'd always loved how the old farmhouse was situated so that from every window she could see the rows of vines thriving in the rich, loamy soil of Central Oregon's Willamette Valley. Her late husband had resented the farm and everything it stood for. Even though Dave had made a success of the land he'd inherited, he'd never been truly happy here. He'd longed for adventure and excitement, not the relentless life of a vintner.

But Jana was content, at least as much as she could be with the turmoil that had always brewed between Dave and Griffin, slowly escalating until she couldn't seem to find a way to bridge the chasm between her husband and their older son.

"I still think about you," he said, although the words were almost swallowed by the cold winter wind that suddenly whipped up from the valley. His graying hair blew across his face as he stared at her, his eyes still the color of the sand where it met the sea. God, those eyes had mesmerized her when she'd been younger. He'd mesmerized her.

"I think about us," he continued. "You're as beautiful as the day we first met, Jana."

She laughed out loud at that bit of ridiculousness. "I'm old, Jim."

"Not to me."

"I hate to break it to you," she said with another laugh. "But you're old too."

The breeze blew again, and she shivered, as much from the cold air as the intensity of his gaze on hers.

"You shouldn't be out here without a coat. Can I come inside?" He stepped closer, his big body blocking the brunt of the wind. He was well over six feet tall, and while the height had made him gangly as a young man, he now seemed perfectly comfortable in his own skin. She found it undeniably attractive. "It's business." He paused then added, "For now."

The door opened behind her, and she turned to find Joey standing at the entrance to the house. He rubbed his eyes with one hand while the other clutched the worn blanket he took everywhere.

"Good morning, sweetheart," she said, stepping away from Jim with a furtive look in his direction.

"It's cold," the boy observed. "You need a coat."

"So I've been told," she murmured. "I'll be inside in a minute. Griffin's in the office next to the kitchen. Do you remember how to get there?"

Joey nodded then said, "I dreamed about Mommy last night. She was an angel."

A lump formed in Jana's throat. "Your mommy is an angel," she confirmed. "She'll always be with you that way."

"I gotta pee." Joey looked around her to where Jim stood, his jaw slack.

"That happens in the morning," Jim confirmed, a confused half smile curving one side of his mouth.

The boy disappeared into the house, slamming shut the door.

"Right now isn't the best time for me," Jana said, reluctantly meeting his curious gaze. "Is it okay if I text you later in the week?"

"Who's the boy?"

She bit down on her lower lip. "It's complicated, Jim, and I'm not sure Griffin wants anyone to know about Joey. He hasn't even told Trevor yet. I'm the only one—"

"Who is he?" The question was more insistent this time.

"The son of Griffin's ex-girlfriend, the one he left town to see." She shook her head. "*See* isn't the right word. Cassie was dying. She asked Griffin to become Joey's guardian."

She watched as Jim sucked in a sharp breath, his expression going blank. It wasn't like him. Normally every emotion he felt played across his strong features. At least that's how she remembered him. What did she really know at this point?

"Surely he's told Maggie about the boy?" He ran a hand through his hair. "She hasn't mentioned anything but—"

"She doesn't know," Jana confirmed. "Like I said—"

"I can't keep this from her. She has a right to—"

"No." Jana crossed her arms over her chest, wishing the ruby-colored turtleneck she wore was thicker. "You can't tell her anything."

"I won't lie to her."

"Then don't say anything."

"A lie of omission," he muttered.

"Please, Jim." She placed a hand on his arm. She could feel the warmth of his skin under his thick jacket. For several moments, they both stared at her hand. She wasn't sure who was more surprised that she'd touched him.

"This has turned Griffin's world upside down," she continued.

"As his leaving did to Maggie's," he insisted.

She squeezed his arm, feeling the muscles under her hand go taut. "He cares about her very much, and I know he wants to make things right. He needs time."

He continued to study her hand, and she pulled it away, self-conscious of the veins that threaded through the top of it. She'd been infatuated with Jim Spencer from the first day she'd arrived in Stonecreek, as a girl of seventeen. He'd been the most intoxicating combination of James Dean cool and Paul Newman sophistication, the scion of the most powerful family in town but also the artistic rebel. For an awkward girl from a barely blue-collar family who just wanted to fit in with the kids at her new high school, he'd been fascinating. Jim didn't care what anyone thought about him. His confidence had drawn her in, and when he'd finally noticed her, she'd been a goner.

"I can't forgive him for hurting her," he whispered, "even if he thinks he had a good reason for it."

"That's understandable. You're a good father."

He glanced up at her, his brows quirking and an almost remorseful look flashing in his eyes. "Not really, but I'm trying."

"It's never too late."

Her breath caught as he took her hand in his, the rough callouses on his palms making heat pool low in her belly.

"I hope you mean that," he whispered.

She yanked her hand away, fisting it at her side. "I need to check on Joey," she said on a rush of air. "And Trevor will be here any minute."

As if on cue, a sleek Porsche appeared around the bend in the long gravel driveway that led to the house.

"Text me later," Jim said. He held the file folder out to her and then turned away once she took it.

Jana swallowed, emotions she'd thought long buried bubbling up inside her as if from a dormant spring brought to life.

She waved to her younger son then took a step back and opened the front door. Griffin appeared in the entry. "Joey's having breakfast. I'd like to tell Trevor about him before they meet." He looked to where Jim was climbing in his old Volvo station wagon and frowned. "Why was he here?"

"I'm commissioning a sculpture for the flower garden next to the tasting room," she said, forcing her voice to come out in a measured tone. "We discussed it before you went to Seattle."

"What did you tell him about Joey?"

"Enough."

"Mom, he can't—"

"He won't say anything to Maggie until you talk to her." She turned to him, cupped his cheek with her palm. "You have to tell her, Griffin."

"You trust him?" His jaw tightened. "He has no reason to keep this secret."

"He will," she said, as sure of Jim's confidence as she was of her own name. "I'm going to sit with

Joey. Talk to Trevor. Make sure he's calm before you two come in again."

Griffin nodded, and Jana walked past him into the house. She closed the door behind her, drew in a shuddery breath and dabbed at the corner of her eye.

It had been a spontaneous decision to invite Jim Spencer back into her life, and now she wondered if she'd opened herself to a second chance or simply unlatched a Pandora's box of renewed trouble and possible heartache.

Maggie jumped at the knock on her door a few nights later. She stood in the kitchen, the only light coming from the glow of her cell phone screen.

The electricity had gone out almost an hour ago, and although it was only eight at night, her house was almost completely dark. The glow of lights from her neighbors' homes shone from beyond the window. Bright strands of Christmas lights outlined the houses, which told her she was the only one affected by the loss of electricity.

But she'd checked the breaker box multiple times and could find nothing wrong.

Whoever was at her door knocked again. She hit the flashlight button on her phone and made her way to the front of the house.

To her shock, Griffin stood on the other side of the door.

He lifted a hand to shade his eyes when she shone the flashlight at him.

"How did you find me?" she asked, lowering the light and casting them both into shadows.

"Don't sound so ominous," he said with a soft laugh.

"I'm serious."

"Morgan was out at Harvest after school today. She mentioned that you'd moved back in here."

"Oh, she and I are going to have a talk," Maggie muttered.

"Was it a secret? It's a small town, Maggie May. I was bound to find out."

"I guess," she agreed reluctantly.

"So…um…" He glanced past her into the house. "I came to bring you a house-rewarming gift." From behind his back, he pulled a ceramic pot that held a Christmas cactus. "Had you gone to bed extra early tonight?"

"My power's out." She took the plant from him, her heart skipping a beat. She'd been so happy to move back to her house, but she was the only one who seemed to think it was a big deal, a step in reclaiming her life.

The fact that Griffin understood made her sad for everything they'd lost.

"Did you check the electrical box?"

"I can't find any tripped breakers," she said with a nod.

"Want me to take a look?"

No. If she let him into her house, she was a little worried she'd end up climbing him like a spider monkey. She might tell herself that she wanted nothing to do with Griffin Stone, but her body clearly hadn't gotten the memo.

It was difficult not to notice how handsome he was in the canvas coat that made his shoulders appear even broader than normal. Stubble darkened his jaw, and although his eyes were still in shadow, she could feel the intensity of his gaze.

"Sure. That would be great."

She lifted the light again and he followed her into the house, through the narrow hall to the staircase that led to the basement.

"Careful, it's steep," she advised, starting to reach out a hand for the railing only to realize she was still holding the plant Griffin had given her.

Turning around, she ran right into the solid wall of his chest.

"I'm going to leave the plant upstairs," she told him, her voice annoyingly breathless.

"Good idea," he murmured and she heard rather than saw his smile.

Between the darkness and her body's reaction to him, Maggie had become totally discombobulated in a matter of minutes. Giving herself an internal lecture on how to not be a ninny, she hurriedly placed the plant on the kitchen table then returned to the top of the stairs.

"I can go down on my own," he offered.

"It's my house." She held her phone up high. "I want to be the one to take care of things."

"Got it." He followed her down the stairs then flipped on the flashlight from his own phone to study the breaker box. "It's a tripped breaker." He flipped the switch, much as she'd done earlier. But now the lights turned back on, leaving Maggie both frustrated and embarrassed.

"I did that," she told him, frowning at the row of switches. "I swear I did that exact thing."

"It hadn't been pushed all the way to the off position before you flipped it on again," he explained. "You'll know for the next time."

"It's still annoying," she grumbled, staring at the breaker box. "But thank you." She glanced up to find Griffin grinning down at her. "What's so funny?"

"You're cute when you're mad." He brushed a strand of hair away from her face. "Actually, you're beautiful all the time. I miss that about you, along with everything else."

Maggie stepped back, flustered as color rushed to her cheeks. "You'll get used to it," she told him and whirled around to escape up the basement steps.

She reached the kitchen and turned off her flashlight then stepped forward to get a better look at the plant he'd brought. It was a perfect size, with delicate red flowers blooming on the ends of several stems.

"I thought you had renters until the spring."

Griffin stood on the opposite side of the kitchen, slowly closing the door to her basement.

"The husband got a job offer in Alabama, where they were from, and the wife wanted to move back there. I was happy to let them break the lease, although I think my dad's actually disappointed I moved out before Christmas."

"He wanted to have the whole family under the same roof for the holidays?"

"I guess." She smoothed a hand along the butcher-block counter she'd loved since childhood. The house had belonged to her grandmother before Maggie bought it, so she'd spend hours here as a girl. In the four years she'd owned it, she'd done little to update things, but that was about to change.

As if reading her mind, Griffin moved toward the oak table, holding up a sample of subway tile. "Remodeling?"

"It's my Christmas present to myself. I'm starting with the bathroom upstairs. It still has the pink toilet my grandma installed when she moved in."

"Who's doing the work?" Griffin asked absently.

"Me," she reported, trying not to fidget when his gaze sharpened on her. "I've checked out lots of tutorials on YouTube and read about a million DIY blogs."

"You're going to renovate a bathroom based on what you've read on the internet?"

She made a face. "Don't be so old-fashioned. You'd be surprised what you can learn online. Plus there's HGTV. Based on the hours of renovation shows I've watched, I'm pretty much an expert."

"Clearly. It's a big job, Maggie."

"I can handle it," she told him. "I have extra time now that the election is over and could use something to keep me…"

He lifted a brow.

"…busy," she finished, crossing her arms over her chest.

"What about the competition for LiveSoft?" he asked, thankfully ignoring the fact that she had so much time on her hands in part because he was no longer in her life.

"I'll manage both."

"Maybe the stuffy CEO will want to help."

"Christian isn't stuffy, and why would he want to help me remodel a bathroom?"

"I got the impression he'd be happy to help you

change a lightbulb or watch paint dry or whatever..."
He scrubbed a hand over his jaw. "He's interested in
you, Maggie."

"He might be moving his entire company here,
Griffin. Of course he's interested in me. I'm the
mayor."

"Not because you're the mayor."

"That's none of your business."

"Maggie."

"I mean it." She threw up her hands. "I told you
we're over. If I want to date someone else...Christian
Milken or Mikey at the barbershop, you have nothing to say about it."

He shrugged. "Mikey's wife might have an opinion."

"You know what I mean."

"Don't date the CEO," he said softly, and the edge
of desperation in his tone shocked her.

"I'm not planning on it," she admitted after a long
moment.

Griffin walked toward her.

"I'm not planning on dating anyone," she said,
pressing a hand to his chest when he'd closed the
distance between them.

"I had to leave." His heartbeat was steady under
her hand as he spoke. Although touching him had
the usual effect of spinning her senses out of control, she couldn't force herself to pull her hand away.
"But I came back."

"For how long?" she asked then pressed her lips
together. She told herself it didn't matter, but that
wasn't true and they both knew it.

"Forever."

He said the word with such conviction it made her heart break all over again. She'd thought she and Griffin were on their way to forever. Then he'd disappeared, and it had taken every bit of strength she had not to fall apart completely.

How could she open herself up to that kind of pain again, no matter how much she wanted to believe he meant it this time?

"You should go," she told him, dropping her hand to her side.

"Maggie." The word was a whispered plea on his lips as he leaned in, his nose almost grazing the sensitive skin of her neck.

"Thank you for the plant," she said, shifting away from him. "And for helping with my breaker." She moved to the kitchen table. "I'm starting demo this weekend, so I need to pack up that bathroom and make sure I have all the tools I need."

"More blogs and YouTube on the docket?"

"Tonight I'm updating my Pinterest board," she told him, earning a small smile.

"I did have something I wanted to talk to you about."

She frowned. In the span of a few seconds, his entire demeanor had changed. He looked sheepish and contrite as he shifted his gaze to the plant he'd brought, like he couldn't quite stand to look her in the eye.

Once again, the urge to offer comfort for whatever was plaguing him rolled through her. But she ignored it. That was simply her being weak, and she was done with weakness.

"Whatever it is won't change things," she said before he could speak.

He was silent for what seemed like an eternity. "Alright then," he said finally, his voice rough. He stepped away from her, and she drew in a deep breath. "Call if you need anything. I understand you want space, but I'll be here if that changes. Always, Maggie."

She inclined her head and he walked out of the kitchen. It took every bit of willpower she possessed not to run after him, but she didn't move. Only lifted a hand to her cheek to wipe away the tears that once again fell.

Chapter Four

For Maggie, the following few days were a whirl-wind of balancing her normal life with managing the aftermath of the latest video uploaded to LiveSoft's social media platforms. The remodeling project had taken a backseat as most of her time was spent an-swering questions about her particular involvement in the decision about a new headquarters. Christian Milken's assistant, who'd filmed the tree lighting, had edited the footage so that it hinted at a possible spark igniting between Christian and Maggie.

While more unwanted attention on her personal life was embarrassing, Maggie had to admit that LiveSoft's followers seemed to love it. Stonecreek had been named one of the two top contenders for the new headquarters. She'd spent the better part of the morning reviewing and responding to comments on the town's Facebook page and Twitter feed, many of which talked about what a cute couple she and Christian would make.

Elsie German from Blush Salon had brought her a basket of skin-care products, to "liven up your complexion" for the next time she'd be on camera. Several other business owners had stopped by to see her, with advice ranging from the length of her skirts to how much lipstick to apply.

In fact, her office had become a revolving door of well-meaning members of the community, all of them excited by the town's chances of winning and annoyingly supportive of her pursuing the charismatic CEO.

"You might want to go shopping for a new bra or two," Irma Cole from The Kitchen restaurant suggested, her smile gleeful. Irma and Grammy had come to talk about plans for the weekend's big event, the annual Stonecreek Christmas pageant. Irma had offered to donate food for the reception after the pageant. She didn't want anyone to be "hangry" while on camera.

Grammy harrumphed from where she sat in the chair across from Maggie's desk. "Don't be ridiculous," Grammy told her longtime friend. "Maggie isn't selling her body to solidify the win."

"Of course not," Irma said with an eye roll. "That would make her a prostitute. Maggie is far too classy for that." She adjusted her own ample cleavage. "But if she likes him, there's no reason she shouldn't have matching lingerie for when things go to the next level. I may be old, but I know men still like some fancy bits when the clothes come off."

"I'll admit you have a point." Grammy pinned Maggie with a stony look. "Do you have nice underwear?"

"I'm not discussing that with either of you," Maggie answered through clenched teeth.

"Even if she didn't get anything new when she was with Griffin," Irma said, ignoring Maggie's affronted tone, "I'm sure she bought nice things for her honeymoon." She glanced at Maggie. "Isn't that right?"

"Still not talking about it," Maggie whispered.

"But you like him," Grammy said, as if it were a predetermined fact. "You agreed to have dinner with him this week."

"We're going to talk about the town," Maggie clarified for what felt like the fiftieth time since she'd mentioned her plans to have dinner with Christian.

"That can't be the only topic you'll discuss," Irma insisted.

"Maybe he'll want to talk about how strange and inappropriate it is that everyone in Stonecreek seems so interested in the two of us dating." She picked up one of the bottles of fancy moisturizer then set it down again.

She couldn't imagine what he thought of the spotlight on his personal life.

"People are excited that we could win," Irma explained, almost apologetically. "And for you to have a new man in your life, of course."

"There's no new man in my life."

How could Maggie consider a new man when she couldn't seem to get over the old one? She'd spent almost every night since Griffin had come to her house dreaming of him. It was as if her heart couldn't let go of him, despite what her brain instructed.

"She's right," her grandmother agreed, rising from her chair. "Mary Margaret's love life is no one's concern but her own. Stonecreek is the best choice for LiveSoft regardless of whether she's dating the CEO or not."

"Thanks, Grammy," Maggie whispered.

Vivian nodded as she walked to the door, gesturing to Irma to follow. "But wear that navy dress with the scoop neck to dinner, dear," she called over her shoulder. "The color makes you look not so washed-out."

Maggie swallowed a shocked laugh. Her grandmother giveth support and her grandmother taketh away.

She should be angry but couldn't quite muster the emotion, understanding why everyone was so invested in Stonecreek winning. It was also difficult to deny that Christian's interest in her was more than simply professional. He'd been texting her regularly, messages that appeared innocuous on the surface but contained a flirty undertone that Maggie wasn't certain how to handle.

It would be easy to fall for a guy like Christian—smart, powerful, handsome and wealthy. Yet even if Maggie hadn't sworn off dating, Christian wouldn't be the man she'd pick.

She had to make it clear that all she could offer was friendship and the promise of life in an amazing town. Surely he'd be fine with that. They barely knew each other. Whatever chemistry people saw between them on social media was a trick of the camera.

Stonecreek would win the competition because it was the right choice, not due to anything she did or didn't do with the CEO.

She opened the drawer to her desk and shoved her new skin-care products into it. Christian and Griffin were meeting at Harvest Vineyard today to discuss environmental sustainability and corporate culture—two subjects they both seemed to find fascinating. Christian had asked her to attend, and although she'd tried to offer excuses, he'd been insistent.

The drive to the vineyard made her heart ache. The last time she'd been out there had been for the hospital gala and after she'd spent the night in Griffin's arms. The landscape looked totally different now, cold and grim and nearly barren. A gray sky loomed above her, perfectly matching her mood. Had Griffin heard the gossip about her and Christian?

She tried to tell herself that she didn't care about his reaction, but that was too big of a lie even for her to swallow.

Panic crested like a wave inside her as she got out of her car. It crashed over her, and she took a step back. The hulking black SUV Christian drove while he was in town sat in the parking lot outside the winery's main office along with Griffin's vintage Land Cruiser.

She thought about the two men, what each might want—what she wanted for herself. The town's expectations and the pressure of making sure everything went according to plan over the next few weeks. It was too much.

Was she really equipped to deal with any of it? She wanted to believe she could handle things. Yet she had difficulty having that kind of confidence in herself. What had she done to earn it?

Instead of heading toward the office where she was due to meet Griffin and Christian, Maggie started down the hill that led to the massive estate vineyard. The temperature had dropped at least ten degrees since she'd left downtown. A fog was quickly descending over the fields, and she could feel the cold to her bones. Zipping up the parka she wore over her wool sweater dress, she kept moving until she was making her way down the rows of dormant vines.

Her tension propelled her forward, like she could outrun her nerves or freeze them from her system. Central Oregon in December was typically rainy, but she could tell from the low-hanging clouds and the fact that she could barely feel her nose that any precipitation they got today would be in the form of snowfall.

As if on cue, a few flakes appeared in the air in front of her. Snow was unusual, so she stopped and tipped up her face, holding out her tongue to feel the snow on it.

"It doesn't taste like nuffin'."

Maggie gave a sharp cry and whirled, shocked to find a solemn-faced boy staring at her from the row next to the one where she stood.

"Snow tastes like water," she said, clasping a hand to her chest.

"My mommy told me snow tasted like cotton candy," he reported, tiny slashes of dark brows furrowing.

Maggie shook her head. "Not so much."

"She also told me she wasn't gonna die," the boy

said, his small voice never wavering. "That was a lie too."

"Oh." Maggie's heart lurched. The pain she felt on this child's behalf chased away her panic more quickly than anything else could have. "I didn't know your mommy, but I bet what she told you was more of a hope than a lie. My mom died when I was fifteen and my sister was only a little older than you at the time. I know it was her greatest hope that she'd find a way to keep living."

"How do you know how old I am?" he asked, ducking under a branch and then between two vines to stand directly in front of her.

"It's the sign on your forehead," she told him then winked when he lifted a hand to his face. "Just kidding. I'm actually pretty good with ages and I'd guess you're around four."

He nodded. "My birthday was in August."

"Mine's in March," she told him. "It's kind of cold today."

"That's why there's snow," he confirmed, kicking a dirt clump with his toe.

"I'm sorry about your mommy. You must miss her very much."

The boy nodded and wiped his nose with the back of one sleeve.

"It's really cold out here, huh?"

Another nod.

"I'm Maggie." She held out her hand. After a moment the boy shook it, his fingers icy cold. "What's your name?"

"Joey," he told her, barely above a whisper.

"Do you live near the vineyard, sweetie? Is your daddy home right now?"

His brow scrunched. "I don't have a daddy." He drew back his hand. "I have Griffin. Mommy gave me to him."

"Oh, my—" Maggie pressed a hand to her mouth. She should have realized it earlier. Griffin had told her he'd gone to Seattle and Cassie had died. Of course, he'd forgotten to mention that he'd become the guardian of his ex-girlfriend's young son.

She straightened as she heard a deep voice calling the boy's name. "Does anyone know you're out here?" she asked.

Joey shook his head. "They were busy."

"Right now they're busy looking for you."

"I like it out here," he told her, kicking the dirt again. "Even when it's cold."

"I understand." She crouched down in front of him. "When my mom died I liked being outside too. The quiet helped me talk to her."

"Yeah," the boy murmured, his eyes seeming to flash with relief at being understood.

"But you have to let a grown-up know where you're going when you leave the house. They get worried otherwise."

Joey seemed to think about that for a moment. "Okay," he agreed, nodding.

"Let's let them know you're okay." She smiled. "Okay?"

"Yeah."

Maggie turned in the direction of the loudest of the voices. "Over here, Griffin," she shouted, taking Joey's hand in hers to begin walking toward the end of the row.

A moment later, Griffin appeared, silhouetted against the creeping fog. "Joey," he shouted and ran forward.

The boy gripped Maggie's hand tighter. "Griffin's mad," he whispered.

"Not exactly mad," Maggie assured him. "He's worried."

"Where the hell have you been?" Griffin demanded of the boy as he came to a stop in front of them.

Joey looked up, giving Maggie an "I told you so" glance that would have made her grandmother proud.

"No swearing," she told Griffin, arching a brow.

His eyes narrowed. "Are you joking right now?"

She squeezed Joey's hand. "We'll talk to Jana about getting a swear jar for the house. Every time he curses, that's a dollar in the swear jar. You get to use the money for whatever you want."

"Really?" Joey asked, his mouth curving into a small smile.

"I promise."

"What are you talking about?" Griffin shook his head. "Joey, you scared Ms. Jana half to death."

The boy's lower lip trembled. "I don't want her to die."

"Griffin." Maggie kept her voice soft but widened her eyes so Griffin would get her message. "You're scaring him," she mouthed above the boy's head.

Griffin closed his eyes and drew in a deep breath. "Joey, I'm sorry." He ran a hand through his hair, making the thick tufts stand on end. He looked wild and desperate and absolutely unsure of what to do next. It melted Maggie's frosty heart.

"I told you," Maggie said to the boy, crouching down again. "Griffin and Ms. Jana were worried. That's why you have to tell someone when you leave the house. In fact, a grown-up needs to go with you if you want to come down to the fields."

"They bury the canes so they don't get cold," the boy said matter-of-factly, reaching out a hand to touch one of the exposed vines.

"I can tell who he's been spending time with," she said, lifting her gaze to Griffin.

His face softened and the glimpse of vulnerability she saw in his eyes there struck to her core.

A gust of wind whipped down the row of vines, making the boy shiver. "Let's get you back to the house," Griffin said, closing the distance between them and lifting the boy into his arms.

Maggie noticed that Joey stayed stiff, unsure of how to relax in Griffin's arms.

She trailed along behind them, trying to wrap her mind around the idea of Griffin as a father figure.

The snow came down heavier, blanketing the fields with a coat of pristine white.

"Will there be enough for a snowman?" Joey asked, unaware of the tension simmering between Griffin and Maggie.

"Maybe," Griffin answered, glancing around at the literal winter wonderland surrounding them. At least a wonderland compared to what they normally experienced in this part of Oregon. "This is what I wanted to talk to you about the other night," he said to Maggie.

Before she could answer, a relieved cry sounded from the top of the hill they were climbing.

"Joey," Jana called on a choked sob as they made their way up. Griffin's mother looked beside herself with worry. She wore a cream-colored turtleneck sweater, dark jeans and worn work boots that came up to her knees. The boots didn't mesh with Jana's otherwise polished appearance, and it made Maggie remember that this woman was tougher than she looked.

Maggie respected Jana for it and liked to think they had that inner strength in common. She drew in a breath, thinking of her near breakdown when she'd first arrived at the vineyard. A few minutes of doubt were manageable. Maybe even normal.

But she'd proven she could handle whatever life handed her. She was infinitely blessed but had also dealt with losses, setbacks and challenges. Each one she'd overcome and she was determined to continue in that vein.

"Maggie found him in the estate vineyard," Griffin reported to his mother as she took the boy from his arms.

"You must be freezing," Jana murmured. Joey wrapped his arms around her neck and buried his face into the soft fabric of her sweater. It was so different from how he'd reacted when Griffin held him.

A quick glance at Griffin's stony features and Maggie realized he was well aware of the boy's contrasting reactions.

"I wanted to check on the grapes," Joey said softly to Jana.

Griffin closed his eyes for a moment. "We should

get him to the house to warm up," he said, his dis-
passionate tone belying the emotions Maggie could
almost see swirling inside him.

"I'll take him," Jana said. "Joey and I can have
hot chocolate while he tells me about his adventure.
You finish the meeting."

At that last word, Maggie looked toward the office to see Christian moving toward them, a scowl
marring his perfect features. The snow had already
stopped, although the air was still bitterly cold for
the valley. She knew most of what Griffin planned
to show Christian was inside the winery, but she
still thought that between the scare with Joey and
the weather, the time wasn't right for the kind of attention the CEO needed.

"We can reschedule," Griffin told his mother.

"He's fine," Jana said gently.

"I want hot chocolate," Joey announced.

"Cancel if you want," Christian called, his hands
shoved deep in his coat pockets. "But this is the only
day I have available." He paused then added, "I'm
heading to Timmins to talk to the city planner over
there. LiveSoft is interested in their environmental
initiatives. Did you know Timmins has the most en-
vironmentally certified buildings per capita than any
other city in Oregon?"

Griffin gave a sharp shake of his head.

Christian glanced toward Maggie. "The town
council has offered to donate a tree to every one of
my employees to increase the community's overall
canopy. Impressive, right?"

"Sure." Maggie grimaced inwardly even as she
tried to keep her emotions from showing on her

face. She understood that Christian was a busy man and LiveSoft had to be his priority, but his reaction seemed insensitive at best.

Going forward with today's meeting had to be the last thing Griffin wanted to do.

"Maybe we could reschedule for next week," she offered, moving to stand next to Griffin. She didn't want him to think she expected him to carry on like he hadn't just had a huge scare.

Christian shook his head, suddenly looking like a petulant schoolboy. "It's now or never."

She swallowed. "Well, then—"

"We'll go over our sustainability initiatives now," Griffin interrupted. He turned to his mother, who was setting Joey on his feet. The main house was situated across a wide swath of snow-covered lawn. "Call if you need anything."

"We'll be fine," she repeated in the way of an experienced mother. Maggie had no doubt Jana would be able to handle Joey with no issues.

Griffin ruffled the boy's hair. "If you want to visit the vines, tell me next time. I'll take you down."

"You were busy," the boy answered, his eyes trained on the ground in front of him.

Crouching down until he was almost at eye level with Joey, Griffin placed a finger under the boy's chin and tipped it up. "I'm never too busy for you. Never."

The boy tilted his head, studying Griffin as if to discern whether he meant the words. After a moment he nodded. "Okay."

Jana took the boy's hand as Griffin straightened again, and they walked toward the house.

"Are you and the kid's mom divorced?" Christian asked when it was just the three of them again.

"Not exactly," Griffin said tightly.

"I get it." Christian nodded. "It's complicated."

Griffin glanced at Maggie. "I hate that word."

She ignored him and instead smiled at Christian. "Did you know Harvest was the first vineyard in Oregon to be certified organic?"

A bit of the impatience in his gaze disappeared. "What made you decide to go that route?"

Griffin was silent for several seconds, and Maggie wondered if he was going to answer the question. Christian might not realize it, but it was clear to her that Griffin couldn't stand the successful CEO.

She cleared her throat and after another moment he said, "This valley is a special place. We want our fields to flourish in harmony with the land and the people who live here. Environmental stewardship is more than just planting trees. Would you like to see the bottling operation?"

"That sounds great."

"Let's head over to the winery."

Maggie hung back, and Griffin turned to her. "Are you coming with us?"

"I'm going to stop in and see Brenna for a minute," she said, forcing a bright smile. "I'll catch up with you."

Griffin's eyes narrowed but his smile remained fixed in place. "Don't be too long." He leaned closer and added in a whisper, "Or I might throttle your CEO boyfriend."

"He's not my—" She shook her head. "Never mind. I won't be long."

She turned and walked into the Harvest office, breathing in the warm, vanilla-scented air. Brenna rose from behind the receptionist desk and walked toward Maggie. "I'm so glad you found Joey. Jana was really worried."

"You knew about him?" Maggie asked, pressing a hand to her stomach. Her shock at finding the boy and gratitude that he was safe were beginning to wear off, anger taking their places inside her heart.

Brenna shook her head, her big brown eyes filled with sympathy. "Of course not. Not until Jana came rushing in here a few minutes before you showed up. I was about to get my coat on to help with the search."

"But he lives in the main house," Maggie whispered. "Marcus runs the vineyard. Did he know?"

Marcus Sanchez was the Harvest Vineyard's CEO. Jana had given him the leadership position after her husband, Dave, died four years ago. Marcus was a soft-spoken man in his late forties. He'd worked at the vineyard for years and had more than earned his place in the business. He had a gift for working the land. Apparently he'd also had a serious crush on Maggie's best friend, Brenna Apria, since she'd come to work in the Harvest office two years ago. It was only after Maggie's aborted wedding that the two of them had connected romantically.

Brenna had known about Trevor's infidelity but hadn't admitted as much to Maggie until the day of the wedding, and her friend's silence had felt like an additional betrayal on top of Trevor's cheating. Maggie had eventually found a way to forgive Brenna, as well as Trevor, and she was sincerely happy Brenna and Marcus were such a perfect fit for each other.

Marcus was sweet and attentive to Brenna. He clearly loved and respected her with his whole heart. Plus he doted on her daughter, Ellie. In fact, much of the reason for him leaving his position at the vineyard was to devote more time to Brenna and Ellie.

"According to Marcus, Griffin didn't tell anyone outside the family. I don't know why."

Maggie tried not to let the pain she felt show on her face, but Brenna wrapped her in a tight hug anyway. "Don't take it personally," her friend whispered.

"How am I supposed to react?" Maggie pulled back. "I tell a man I love him and a few days later he ghosts me then returns and asks for another chance but doesn't bother to mention that he's now the guardian to a four-year-old boy."

"Yikes," Brenna murmured. "When you say it like that, it's not so great."

"It's worse than that." Maggie sighed. "I need to get out there. Griffin doesn't like Christian—"

"Because Christian likes you."

"Among other reasons," Maggie admitted. "But let's take my mind off my mess of a life for a quick second and talk about your wedding." Brenna and Marcus were getting married on New Year's Eve then leaving on an extended honeymoon through Europe, taking Ellie along with them.

"Your dress will be in tomorrow if you can squeeze in a fitting."

"Squeeze being the operative word with all of the catered holiday events I've been attending lately." Maggie smiled. "I'm so excited for you, Brenna."

"Me too." Brenna beamed, happiness radiating from her. Maggie was only a teensy bit jealous and reminded herself that Brenna had been through so much before finding her happily-ever-after.

"I'll text you in the morning and we can meet at the dress shop if that works?"

Brenna nodded. "Ellie will want to come too. She's so excited that the two of you are going to be in matching dresses."

"I'm going to be upstaged by a kid," Maggie said with a laugh then glanced at her watch. "I need to go."

"Are you really going to join their meeting? Can you imagine the amount of testosterone flying through the winery at the moment?"

"That's the plan but..." Maggie pressed the heel of her palm to her forehead. "I'm not sure if I can face either of them."

"I'll handle it," Brenna said, squeezing her hand. "I can tell Griffin you got an emergency call about something in town and had to drive back."

"Thank you," Maggie whispered. "I need a little time to process...well...everything."

Brenna hugged her. "It's fine, sweetie."

Maggie walked out into the cold, glancing toward the winery. The Craftsman-style building looked tranquil in the snow. A central corridor drawing visitors toward the tasting room situated to the west and overlooking the main vineyard separated two wings that contained barrel storage. Looks could be deceiving, Maggie thought as she headed for her car. It might be wimpy of her to take off, but she'd have plenty of time to deal with both Griffin and Christian over the next couple of weeks. An escape was exactly what she needed right now.

Chapter Five

"Maybe I'll just wait out here." Griffin eyed the dress boutique then met Marcus's amused gaze. "Seriously. I'm fine to wait."

"Don't be a chicken," Marcus told him, making little squawking noises.

"That's rude," Griffin muttered.

"It's freezing. The dress shop is warm."

That much was true. The weather had stayed in the high twenties and yesterday's snowfall had yet to melt off.

"Besides," Marcus continued, "Ellie will want you to see her dress."

Griffin smiled even as he shook his head. Marcus's soon-to-be stepdaughter was an adorable bundle of energy. The girl had been a regular visitor to the Harvest office ever since Marcus and Brenna became an official couple. Griffin hoped that one day Joey would be as lively and outgoing as Brenna's six-year-old daughter, although it seemed doubtful with everything the boy had been through.

They'd had another rough night of sleep so Joey was napping now. Griffin's mom had been happy to stay at the house while Griffin drove into town. He'd met with two preschool directors, trying to determine the best fit for Joey, who would start attending school in the New Year. Both had advised him that a routine would be good for the boy, although panic speared through Griffin at the thought of leaving Joey with anyone but Jana. Did all parents have these kinds of nerves? Could Griffin really consider himself the boy's parent?

His heart stammered at the thought.

"It's a dress boutique," Marcus said, giving him a curious look. "Not a torture chamber."

"Understood." Griffin followed him into the store. The little bells above the door jingled and it was like entering an alternate universe. He'd grown up in Stonecreek and thought he knew the town like the back of his hand, but he'd managed to avoid Something New Boutique for all of his thirty years on the planet.

A world dominated by a million shades of white enveloped him. From the racks of dresses lining the walls to painted furniture that looked so delicate he'd be afraid to sit down, to the decorative chandeliers and oversize mirrors and a huge vase of flowers in the center of a table that seemed to serve as the store's register counter, everything was white or off-white or cream colored or… How could there be so many white hues?

"Wow," Marcus murmured.

"You're rethinking the torture aspect, aren't you?" Griffin asked under his breath.

"Marcus, look at me." Ellie's gleeful shout broke the quiet as she came dashing out from behind a heavy curtain. She was a shooting star of color, her dress a deep ruby that looked almost brilliant against the store's neutral palette. It was shiny satin with lace cap sleeves and an overlay studded with tiny crystals. She looked adorable and ecstatic to be showing off her gown.

"You're a princess," Marcus told her, grinning widely. The girl jumped into his arms. "The most beautiful girl I've ever seen."

"Is that so?" Brenna followed her daughter, one brow quirked.

"And you're the most beautiful woman," Marcus answered without hesitation.

"Smooth," Griffin muttered. He turned to greet Brenna and froze, his mouth going dry as his heart began to gallop in his chest.

She'd opened the curtain all the way to reveal Maggie standing in front of a full-length mirror, wearing a dress the same color as Ellie's but in a far more mature style. It was strapless, the rich hue making her skin look luminous, and seemed to highlight the rich color of her dark hair. The dress was fitted to her waist and the curve of her hips before flaring near the hem.

Her gaze met his in the mirror, and her cheeks went bright pink. She sucked in a breath and for a moment he saw every emotion that raced through her reflected in her gray eyes. Pain…need…hope…desire…disappointment. The last one pierced his heart. He'd never wanted to hurt her, but there was no denying he had.

"Something you forgot to mention?" he asked Marcus.

"Someone actually," his friend corrected. "You can thank me later."

Brenna put a hand on his arm. "I haven't had a chance to talk to you since we learned about Josy."

Griffin's gaze darted to Maggie, who quickly pulled shut the curtain.

"I meant to tell everyone." He met Brenna's sympathetic gaze once again. "It was wrong, but I didn't know how to talk about it."

"I understand," she told him with a gentle squeeze. "Maggie will get there too."

He bit off a gruff laugh. "Are you sure?"

She shook her head. "No, but I'm hopeful."

"Yeah," he said with a sigh. "Hope isn't something I'm used to relying on."

"Don't give up." She smiled again as she looked over to where Marcus was dancing with Ellie, the girl laughing as he swung her around. "Selfishly, I'm glad you're back. Marcus feels a lot better about stepping away from the day-to-day operations at the vineyard with you on board to take over."

"It's still hard for me to believe. My dad is probably rolling over in his grave."

"From what your mom has told me, I doubt that's true."

Griffin gave a good-natured eye roll. "She's a fan of hope, as well."

"Ellie, time to change back into your regular clothes."

"I like the dress," her daughter said, crossing her arms over her thin chest.

"The child has good taste." An older woman, who Griffin assumed must be the saleslady or owner of the boutique, emerged from behind the curtain, the dress Maggie had been wearing draped over her arm. "Just like her mother."

"Not another word." Marcus held up his hands. "I don't want to know anything about my beautiful bride's dress until our wedding day."

"Mommy's going to look real pretty," Ellie told him.

"Of course she is," he agreed without reluctance.

His phone rang and he pulled it out of his pocket. "I need to take this call. Ellie, if you take off the dress, we'll stop for ice cream on the way to the vineyard."

The girl squealed her agreement then followed Brenna behind the curtain. Marcus stepped outside to take his call and the saleslady walked into a back room with Maggie's dress. That left Griffin alone to—

"How's Joey?"

He drew in a breath as Maggie appeared and closed the distance between them.

"He has nightmares and sometimes I hear him crying when he's supposed to be brushing his teeth. We're seeing a therapist tomorrow." He shrugged. "On the plus side, he has a great appetite."

"It will get better."

"I'm sorry you found out that way," he said quietly.

"What happened to no apologies?" Her fingers played with the delicate amber pendant around her neck.

"That was a stupid suggestion on my part." He lifted a hand to reach for her then thought better of it. He hadn't earned the right to touch her again, no matter how much he wanted to. "Along with the belief that I could get through life without complications."

"I can guarantee that's not going to happen when you're raising a child," she said with a sad smile.

"It wasn't going to happen anyway," he answered. "But Joey is way more than a complication."

"I'm sure it meant a lot to Cassie that you were willing to take him."

"She didn't give me much of a choice," he admitted ruefully. "I tried to convince her she could find someone more suited for the task, but at this point he belongs to me. He's been through too much and needs some stability."

"Griffin Stone offering stability," Maggie murmured. "Who would have ever thought it?"

"I'm not sure I would have known I'm capable of handling it without these past few months and you in my life."

She dropped her gaze, the corners of her gorgeous mouth turning down into a slight frown. "Don't say that."

"It's true, Maggie. I can't imagine how I'll keep going without you."

"You already are."

"Have I told you today that I miss you?"

She shook her head, snagging her bottom lip between her teeth.

"That you're beautiful and smart and I don't deserve another chance but want one so much it hurts."

"Stop," she whispered. "It doesn't change anything. You can't use the boy to manipulate my emotions."

"Ouch." Griffin massaged the back of his neck, trying to absorb the sting of her words. "I'm not trying to do that. Joey is here. He's mine. My life has been turned upside down this past month. You're the only part of it that I never questioned."

"Except you did." She met his gaze and he hated that he'd been the one to put the shadow in her eyes.

"I've messed things up. I get that. But I can change." He cleared his throat. "I *have* changed."

"Griffin."

"Can we at least be friends, Maggie? Don't shut me out completely."

Her full lips pressed into a thin line but after a moment she nodded. "Friends."

Before he could thank her, the door to the boutique opened and Marcus came back in. "Maggie, I hear things are going well with LiveSoft."

She smiled. "We're in the finals. It will be a whirlwind before the holidays, but everyone is pitching in. We have the pageant and the historic home tour this weekend. Christian and a few key employees from the company will be here. The hope is that they fall in love with the town and see their futures here."

"No pressure," Marcus said with a laugh.

"Right?" She shook her head, glancing at Griffin, her brows pinching slightly.

"With you leading Stonecreek, there's no doubt the town will win," he told her.

She sighed. "I wish I had your confidence. But if we aren't chosen, it won't be for lack of trying. Actually, I'm late to meet Miles to talk about available real estate. Would you tell Brenna and Ellie I said goodbye?"

"You bet," Marcus answered.

"I can walk you to his office," Griffin offered, already moving toward the door.

"I know the way," she said, shaking her head. "I'll talk to everyone later."

He watched her leave, pain splitting his chest.

"She'll come around," Marcus said, sounding much like Brenna had earlier.

"I messed up royally," Griffin muttered. "You have no idea."

Marcus inclined his head toward the dressing room. "Those two gave me back my heart. After my divorce, I went on autopilot and lived like that for years. I'd given up on life having meaning outside of work. One look at Brenna and everything changed. Then I met Ellie and there was no going back." He shrugged. "She didn't want to take a chance on me, but I knew we were meant to be together. She was my one."

Griffin drew in a deep breath. "Maggie is the only woman I've ever truly loved. I won't find anyone else. I don't want to try."

"Be patient with her."

"Not my strong suit."

"Is she worth it?"

"Yes," Griffin answered, an unfamiliar sense of

peace settling in his chest. Maggie was worth waiting for no matter how long it took. And if she never gave him the chance he yearned for, he'd find a way to be grateful for the time he'd had with her.

Ellie ran out from the dressing room and Marcus automatically bent to scoop her up once again. After everything Joey had been through, Griffin wondered if he'd ever see that kind of pure joy on the boy's face. He had his doubts but knew for certain he'd do everything in his power to make it so.

"Hello?" Jana pushed open the door to the detached studio that sat behind the Spencer house on a tree-lined street north of downtown Stonecreek. "Jim?"

There was no answer so she walked in without an invitation. His Volvo was parked in the driveway and they'd scheduled a time to meet so he must be around somewhere.

Her heart leaped to her throat when she caught sight of him, a pair of wireless headphones over his ears which explained why he hadn't heard her knock.

The studio was bright, if cluttered, with high windows and skylights on the north side. The ceiling was vaulted, and in addition to the door she'd entered, there was a wide warehouse-type door at the far end. The walls were cream colored and mostly unadorned. Along with the main studio space, she could see two other smaller rooms, one that looked like an office and another that appeared to function as a storage room.

Jim stood in front of a large stand that held an enormous hunk of clay, using his hands and metal tools he grabbed from a nearby tool chest to shape his creation. The scene reminded Jana of the first time she'd seen him. Her family had just moved to Stonecreek so she'd been new to the high school, trying to navigate her way through a student population who had, for the most part, known each other since grade school. At that time, the town was smaller and the community even more tight-knit. She'd gone looking for her English teacher after school, needing to get caught up on a reading assignment. In the empty classroom, she'd stumbled upon a boy at the chalkboard—back in the day when they still relied on old-fashioned chalk.

He was tall and lanky, his thick brown hair grazing his shoulders in a way that was both rebellious and ultrasexy. He'd been sketching on the board, swirling shapes and geometric designs. The chalk squeaked and clicked as he worked, his arm moving at a furious pace like he was possessed by some fiery need to release the creativity bottled up inside him.

She'd been mesmerized, moving closer, drawn toward him by some invisible string. Then she'd tripped over the leg of a desk chair and the stack of books in her arms had tumbled to the floor.

The boy turned, his arm still lifted, and his gaze crashed into hers. She'd never seen anything like the mix of passion and desperation in his eyes. In that moment, Jana had fallen hopelessly in love with Jim Spencer.

Although decades older now, his body remained muscled. He'd moved on from sketching and painting to sculpture. The change in medium suited him.

She could tell he was in his element as he concentrated on the work in front of him.

He wiped at his brow with the back of one arm then stilled and slowly turned toward her.

She pointed a finger at her ear and he stripped off the headphones, the tinny sound of classical music filling the studio.

"Sorry," she said automatically. "I didn't mean to interrupt." He tapped on the phone sitting on top of the tool chest, and the music stopped. "I swear I didn't make a sound."

"White musk," he said, flipping on the water at the utility sink to wash his hands.

"Excuse me?"

"Your perfume," he clarified. "It's the same one you've worn for years."

She felt color rise to her cheeks. When was the last time she'd blushed? "I read somewhere that a woman needs a signature scent so I've never deviated." She laughed, surprised at how breathless she sounded. "Or perhaps I'm just boring."

"Not boring," Jim told her with a half smile. The curve of his lips had always made her knees go weak, but it had been years since he'd smiled at her like that. They'd both done a bang-up job over the years of being civil but never really interacting. It hadn't been difficult. Jana spent most of her time at the vineyard, and Jim tended to become consumed with whatever piece of art he was working on at the moment.

"I like your space," she said when the weight of his stare became too much for her to bear.

He glanced around the room as if seeing it through her eyes. "Things are a mess." He pointed to stacks of papers shoved into one corner. "I need to organize and catalog but it's not my priority."

"I could help," she blurted then immediately regretted it when Jim gave her a look of pure shock. "You probably don't want help. It's not a big deal."

"It is," he countered softly. "I never let anyone help in the studio. My art is the most personal thing I have." He shrugged. "It sounds petty now, but this place was the only thing I ever had that felt like it truly belonged to me. When the kids were little, I kept the door locked because I didn't want them to mess with anything. Even Charlotte rarely came in here."

Jana drew in a breath at the mention of Jim's deceased wife. She hadn't known Charlotte Spencer well. The other woman had been a couple of years younger than Jana and part of the "in crowd," unlike Jana. Charlotte's father was a prominent surgeon in town. The family ran in the same country-club crowds as the Spencers. Unlike Jana. It was hard to believe that a town the size of Stonecreek would have such a social hierarchy, but it did then just as it did now. Charlotte had always been at the top of it and because of that, Vivian Spencer had thought her to be the perfect wife for her beloved only son.

Unlike Jana.

Of course, none of Jana's uncharitable feelings toward Charlotte were actually founded. She'd always been kind, if quiet. An introvert happy to devote her life to raising her three children and taking care of her absentminded husband.

"I understand." Jana forced a smile even though she felt like a naive little fool for suggesting he'd want her intrusion into this private space. "Honestly, I'm just looking for something to fill my time. Joey is going to start preschool after the break and I want to give Griffin space as he takes over at Harvest. Nothing like having Mom looking over your shoulder when you're a grown man and—"

"I'd like for you to help," Jim interrupted.

She placed a hand on her heated cheek. "So I stop babbling?"

He chuckled. "You're looking at the new and improved Jim Spencer. I'm trying hard to change from the selfish jerk I've been for years."

"You were never that," she whispered.

"We both know I was." His brows furrowed. "Although you know me more as spineless. A man who couldn't stand up to his mother."

"You were still a boy back then."

"It doesn't excuse how I treated you." He took a step closer. "I'm sorry, Jana."

She forced a laugh, waved a hand in front of her face as if to brush off his comments then pulled it to her side when it was clear her fingers were trembling. "There's no reason for you to apologize. We were young. Things didn't work out. We've both gone on to have great lives."

"Yes," he agreed but his gaze remained intense on hers. "But do you ever think about what might have been?"

"Oh, no." She took a step away from him, needing more distance. Wanting to turn tail and run. "That wouldn't be helpful to anyone. I loved Dave and you were happy with Charlotte. Things worked out the way they were meant to." She nodded, trying to convince herself as much as him. "We can be friends now, Jim, but we aren't the people we used to be."

"Thank God for that in my case," he muttered.

"You're too hard on yourself." She inched closer again, the invisible pull between them drawing her in. "You have a career, three wonderful children—"

"Maggie practically raised Morgan and Ben after Charlotte died. I retreated into myself and it's taken me years to come out of that."

"Everyone deals with grief in their own way."

"You never would have ignored your boys the way I did my kids. It's my deepest regret."

His voice was hollow yet filled with so much pain. She reached for him, placing her hand on his arm. "I made plenty of mistakes. I might have been present for my sons, but I also stood by and watched my husband and Griffin try to tear each other apart. I could have—should have—stepped in to stop it, but I didn't. Maybe Dave would have gotten past his anger, or at least stopped taking out his resentment on our son."

"That was on him," Jim told her. "Not you."

"I could have made it better if—" She broke off as guilt and regret swamped her. Jim wrapped his strong arms around her and she rested her head against his chest, taking comfort in his steady heartbeat.

"We're quite a pair," he whispered.

She glanced at him from under lashes, and the tenderness in his gaze chased away all the pain encircling her heart.

Then he kissed her. Her breath caught in her throat as his lips brushed across hers, both soft and firm. The kiss felt new and at the same time familiar, a homecoming to a place she'd never been before. She splayed her hands across his chest, reveling in the moment. His heat enveloped her, and she could smell a heady mix of his soap and the earthy scent of clay.

She wanted to stay like this forever, but Jim pulled away suddenly. She reached out a hand to steady herself then went stiff at the sound of Maggie's voice behind her.

"Dad? Jana? What's going on?"

Jim blinked, opened his mouth to explain but no words came out. So Jana schooled her features and turned with a smile.

"Hey, Maggie. Your dad and I were meeting about the commission he's doing."

Maggie crossed her arms over her chest. "Really?"

Jana licked her lips and nodded. "Yes. I'm also going to help him clean up the studio a bit." She grabbed a small stack of papers from a bookshelf situated on one wall. "Organization is my strong suit."

"That should make you happy, Mags," Jim said. "You've been wanting me to take care of the mess in here for years."

"True," Maggie agreed with a slow nod. "Although I'm surprised you've finally agreed to it."

"Jana is very convincing," Jim murmured, and Jana felt color flood her cheeks again. She was blushing in front of the woman who'd dated both of her sons.

Maggie glanced between the two of them a few more seconds then said, "Do you remember we're going to the junior high band concert tonight?" She looked at Jana. "It's Ben's first year in the jazz ensemble."

"Good for him," Jana said quickly. "Trevor was in the band. I used to love the holiday programs."

"You're welcome to join us," Jim offered, stepping forward and pressing a hand to the small of her back.

She saw Maggie's eyebrows go up.

"I appreciate the offer, but I should be getting back to home. Griffin took Joey with him on some errands. I'd like to be there when they return."

Jim nodded. "How's he doing?"

"You know about the boy?" Maggie's tone was rife with accusation. "I never mentioned it."

Jana closed her eyes for a moment and heard Jim sigh. "Your father came to the vineyard last week for a meeting. It was only a few days before you met Joey."

"By accident," Maggie said.

"My introduction was about the same." Jim ran a hand through his hair, the same nervous gesture he'd had since they were young.

"Don't be angry with your dad," Jana pleaded. "I made him promise not to say anything until Griffin had a chance to tell you."

"Had a chance," Maggie muttered. "We both know that isn't how it went."

"You have to understand how difficult this has been for him."

"Perhaps if he'd told me about—" Maggie stopped, shook her head. "It's fine. Griffin made his choice, and I made mine."

"I love my son," Jana told her. "But he's made some doozy-level mistakes. How he left things with you was the biggest. I had such a great time working with you on the hospital benefit. I hope that what's between—or no longer between—you and Griffin doesn't change our…" she paused, offered a smile "…our friendship."

To her relief, Maggie returned her smile. "Of course not. I'm sure Griffin and I will end up friends of a sort, eventually. Stonecreek is too small a town to have a breakup rule your life."

Jim's hand dropped from her back, but Jana kept her smile in place. "You're way smarter than I ever was, Maggie," she said. She glanced up at Jim but didn't meet his gaze. "We seem to keep getting distracted, but I'm looking forward to talking to you about the commission."

"How about lunch tomorrow in town?" he asked.

Not a date, she reminded herself, when her heart seemed to skip a beat. A business lunch. "That would be fine. I'll meet you at The Kitchen at noon."

Without waiting for an answer, she said goodbye to Maggie and walked out, suddenly overwhelmed by both the present moment and the feelings she'd buried for so long that rose up inside her.

Chapter Six

Griffin pulled up outside Maggie's house just before midnight on Friday, glancing into the backseat of his Land Cruiser as he turned off the ignition.

"You should be asleep."

Joey blinked at him, his dark eyes bright and wide. "I'm not tired."

The boy had gone to bed almost two hours earlier, after a bath and several stories. Griffin had congratulated himself on mastering a bedtime routine and had gone into his father's old office to continue reviewing vineyard files after his mom went to her room to read. He still had so much to catch up on as far as running Harvest.

He'd been shocked to see Maggie's number pop up on his phone, both due to the late hour and because she'd been so sure when she told him she needed space.

Her frantic voice at the other end of the line had made his gut tighten, although thankfully the emergency had just been a broken pipe. He'd instructed her on turning off the main water supply to her house over the phone then immediately offered to come by and help her fix the issue.

It was obvious she didn't want his assistance but had reluctantly agreed when he'd insisted, reminding her that she was going to have a hard time finding a local plumber to come before morning. He'd walked out of the office to gather his tools and tell his mom he was heading out, only to find Joey sitting in the hallway, his bony knees gathered to his chest.

So much for mastering bedtime.

Griffin had tried to convince the boy to go to bed—using every trick he'd learned in the dozens of parenting articles he'd read since Cassie died.

Joey could have cared less about Griffin's armchair expertise.

He'd thought about simply walking out, but after the little disappearing act in the fields he figured that wasn't a great idea. The last thing he needed was a search party at midnight with the temperatures hovering near freezing.

His mom hadn't blinked an eye when he'd explained the situation, proving that he'd indeed turned their lives so totally upside down that very little could shock her at this point.

Clearly he'd done the same to Maggie, whose face went slack for only a moment before she smiled down at Joey and stepped back to allow them both into her house. She wore faded jeans and a damp and dusty University of Oregon T-shirt, her long hair pulled back into a messy bun. It was the polar opposite of how she appeared recently, poised and polished in her role as mayor. The glimpse behind her public mask did crazy things to his insides.

"Joey couldn't sleep," Griffin said under his breath. "I tried to convince him but—"

Joey turned and gave him a look that could only be described as withering. "I can hear you."

"Would you like a glass of warm milk or something to eat?" Maggie asked the boy, helping him out of his winter coat.

"I'm going to watch Griffin," Joey answered. "I don't know whether I'm going to be a winemaker or a plumber when I grow up." He paused then added, "Or maybe a firefighter."

Maggie ruffled his hair. "All noble professions." She hung the coat on a rack in the corner of the entry then held out a hand to Griffin. "May I take your coat as well?"

He shrugged out of the heavy canvas jacket and handed it to her, shifting his toolbox from one hand to the other.

"Does it stink?" Joey asked, stepping forward and pressing his nose to the sleeve of Griffin's coat.

"No, of course not," Maggie said quickly. "I just…"

"You smelled it," Joey told her. "A big whiff."

Griffin frowned as color rose to her cheeks.

"It smells like Griffin," she whispered after a moment.

"He doesn't stink," Joey reported. "Unless he's gone for a run."

"That's true," she agreed then gave Griffin a tight

smile. "Why don't I show you where I'm having the problem?"

He nodded, deciding against commenting on the fact that she'd just sniffed his jacket. But a tiny glimmer of happiness bubbled up inside him. She might not want to like him at the moment, but she still liked the way he smelled. He was desperate enough to see that as a win.

Besides, she'd called him and agreed to let him come over to help. He couldn't imagine Captain CEO handling a busted pipe.

He followed her and Joey up the stairs and through her bedroom. The room was decorated in shades of pale blue and off-white, soothing colors for a space that seemed like a sanctuary. The furniture was crafted from blond wood and looked antique, but the thick cover on the bed and the white plantation shutters that adorned the window offset it with a modern feel.

"Whoa," Joey breathed as they walked into the adjoining bathroom. "This place is a mess."

"I was doing demo," Maggie explained then added, "I'm behind on my timeline so I might have gotten a little overzealous."

"I'd say so." Griffin stepped into the space behind Joey, sliding a hand across his jaw as he surveyed the damage. The bathroom was a decent size, especially for a house that was at least fifty years old. It looked like she'd started with the walls, as piles of crumbling tile littered the floor. "Not a fan of salmon-colored tile I take it?"

"It's like they stuck it to the walls with super glue.

I couldn't get the tiles to come off, and it made me really mad."

"The adhesive is meant to last."

"After a while, I thought it would be easiest to take down the whole wall. Even when I managed to pry off a tile, the wall behind it was damaged so…"

"Not a bad idea," Griffin said with a nod. "But you have to be careful not to hit the water lines."

"Great tip." Maggie rolled her eyes. "Thanks to you I managed to turn off the water to the house before I flooded the whole place. But now I can't even flush the toilet."

"Don't go number two then," Joey advised. "That's gross."

Griffin laughed softly and was happy to see Maggie smile at the boy's comment. Then she pressed a finger to the corner of one eye with a sniff, and he realized how upset the mistake had made her.

"We'll figure it out," he promised.

Her smile went slightly brittle at the edges. "I can stay with my dad again if I need to. He doesn't even know I'm tackling the remodeling on my own."

Griffin stepped over the piles of fragmented tile and cracked plaster.

"It looks like you hit the hot water supply line for the shower. I'll need to cut the pipe and we're going to cap it off so you can turn the water back on to the rest of the house. You'll need a plumber to repair the shower before it's able to be used again."

Her chin trembled slightly as she stared at the broken pipe. "Thank you," she whispered. Griffin couldn't quite understand her reaction to the mistake. Her dismay seemed out of proportion for how simple it would be to fix.

"Can I have a snack now?" Joey asked, lifting a hand to cover his yawn. "And watch TV? I don't think I want to be a plumber. I forgot about number two."

Maggie nodded, her smile firmly back in place. "Sure, sweetie."

"I need to grab a few things from the Land Cruiser." Griffin ruffled the boy's hair. "I won't be long."

They filed out of the bathroom and Griffin headed for the front door as Maggie led Joey to the kitchen.

By the time he returned from gathering the rest of the tools he needed, she was settling Joey on the couch, a cartoon playing on the flat-screen television.

"I can handle it if you want to change into clean clothes," he told her when she met him at the bottom of the stairs.

"It's my house," she said firmly. "I want to learn how to take care of it."

He wanted to grin at the determined glint in her gray eyes but had a feeling she wouldn't appreciate that at all. Her resolve only made him admire her more.

Admire. What an insufficient word to describe everything he felt for Maggie. Admiration, yes. Desire. Need. Longing. Lov—

No. He wouldn't allow himself to go there again. Not yet. He understood how badly he'd messed up. He needed to earn his place in her life. Tonight was an opening that he'd gladly take. He wouldn't push her.

"That's a smart idea," he said and turned to the stairs.

"You think I'm in over my head," she said quietly when they were surveying the debris once more. "I can't do it on my own."

"I never said that."

"But you're thinking it." She gave a humorless laugh. "Heck, *I'm* thinking it. With everything else going on right now plus Christmas around the corner, this wasn't the time for a home renovation project. Especially when I know nothing about home renovations."

"What inspired the remodel?" He arched an eyebrow. "Too many binge sessions of HGTV?"

"Maybe," she admitted with a genuine smile then shrugged. "Those people get a lot done in an hour, even with commercials."

"True," he agreed, handing her a pipe cutter. "I brought everything you need based on how you explained the problem over the phone. You're going to cut out the damaged ends of the pipe and then we'll solder on a copper cap."

"With a blow torch?"

He lifted the welding tool. "We're not making crème brûlée with this thing."

She looked dubious but followed his instructions and within a half hour and one check-in on Joey, the pipe had been capped.

"That was kind of awesome," she said as she stepped back to survey her work.

"You did great."

"I started this to have something of my own." She bit down on her lower lip, sending another shockwave of awareness through Griffin. He tamped it down.

This was the friend zone, and he wasn't going to let his lust muck it up.

"You bought the house from your grandmother," he pointed out. "It belongs to you."

Maggie nodded then shook her head. "Yes, but in the four years I've owned it, nothing has changed. I haven't made anything personal. Most of the furniture, other than the bedroom, belonged to her. It's just like my job."

"Being mayor?"

"I followed in her footsteps, and although I was elected to that first term, it felt more like I'd inherited the position."

He put away the tools. "Your re-election changed that?"

"I thought so. During the campaign, I stepped out of her shadow. So much happened this year. I wasn't very popular when I walked away from my wedding."

"Trevor wasn't the most well-liked guy after it came out that he'd cheated."

"But we both shook off some of the expectations of our families and this town after the scandal. I had big plans for Stonecreek. I still do." She sighed. "Instead of working on those goals, my focus has been smiling and playing hostess for the LiveSoft campaign."

"Are you having second thoughts about trying to bring the company here?"

"Not at all. It's a growing company with tons of potential that's a perfect fit for the town. It would be a huge win for Stonecreek, but it feels like the competition is more about me doing a song and dance for Christian. No one is focusing on the substantive piece—the town as a whole is the right choice."

"I don't spend much time on social media, but from what I've seen substance is in short supply."

"It's all part of the game." She ran her hand along the edge of the vanity's pink marble top. "I get that. This town means so much to me. I'd do almost anything for Stonecreek, but tearing out old tile was for me. Does that make sense?"

"Yes," he said slowly, "although some people would argue a pedicure or sitting down with a good book would also be a way to treat yourself."

She picked up a tiny piece of broken tile and lobbed it at him, sticking out her tongue. "Some women get pedicures. I knock down walls."

"Good to know," Griffin said with a chuckle. "The town is lucky to have you, Maggie May."

"Thanks," she whispered.

"I was lucky to have you." He cursed himself when she looked away.

"Tell me about Joey coming with you tonight." She brushed at the front of her T-shirt like that would take care of the dust and grime covering it.

"Nighttime is tough for him. Sometimes the nightmares wake him, but tonight he couldn't fall asleep. I could have forced him to stay with my mom but he's my responsibility."

She looked up at him and flashed a small smile. "He's lucky to have you."

Suddenly the air between them was charged with the same electric connection he'd felt the moment he'd laid eyes on her hurrying along the sidewalk in a wedding dress six months ago. He could never have imagined the changes that had occurred in his life since returning to Stonecreek and what an important part of it Maggie would become.

She licked her lips, and he nearly groaned. Instead of letting his body take the lead, Griffin picked up his toolbox and shrugged. "I should go check on him."

Maggie blinked several times then nodded. "Sure."

She led the way back downstairs, and they found Joey curled up on the sofa, fast asleep.

"He's really adorable," she murmured. "I hate what he's been through."

"Me too." Griffin ran a hand through his hair. "Cassie was a great mom. It's still difficult for me to believe she's gone. I can't imagine how he feels. The therapist says we need to address his anxiety and keep giving him love and reassurance so he begins to feel safe again."

"You're taking him to see someone?"

"Cassie already had a therapist in Seattle. She and the pediatrician here both recommended the same person. Do you know Lana James? She's a few years older than my mom so I think she's been around for a while."

Maggie put a hand to her chest. "She's who Morgan, Ben and I saw after Mom died. Grammy set it up. She'd just started her practice. There were only a few sessions, but it helped. She helped."

"I didn't think about the fact that you and Joey had that kind of loss in common. You were fifteen when your mom died, right?"

She nodded and looked up at him, her beautiful eyes sad but clear. "He and I talked about it when I found him in the fields. Morgan was his age. If you think it would help, I'm sure she'd be happy to talk to him. She's on a better path now and is great with kids."

"Really?" The viselike band that'd had Griffin's heart in a stranglehold for the past six weeks loosened the tiniest bit. He knew he wasn't alone in all this, but for Maggie to get involved gave him a different kind of hope. "I should probably talk to Dr. James first, make sure she thinks Joey could handle it."

"Of course."

"Thank you, Maggie. That…um…" He cleared his throat when his voice cracked. Griffin wasn't used to feeling…well…this much emotion. The woman standing next to him had changed everything. "That means a lot."

She reached out and placed a hand on his arm, a gentle touch that he felt to his core. "If you're going to stay in Stonecreek," she told him, "you better get used to accepting help. I know that lone wolf thing is all hot and sexy, but we're a pack community around here." She inclined her head toward the boy sleeping on the sofa. "And you're raising a child. You're going to be coaching little league in a year or two if you don't watch out."

He leaned closer and nudged her shoulder. "You might need to repeat that last bit. I got caught on the part where you think I'm hot and sexy."

She laughed, poking him in the ribs before stepping away. "And incorrigible."

"In case I haven't mentioned it before, I find five-syllable words vociferously sexy."

"You have an indefatigable spirit," she said with a wink.

"Six?" He held up his hands, palms out. "Now you're just showing off."

She touched the bun on the back of her head and grimaced. "Look at me. I'm about the least sexy I've ever been."

"Eye of the beholder," he whispered, reaching out to tuck a loose lock of hair behind one ear.

Her eyes darkened and that crazy charge between them sparked to life again. She swayed toward him, and Griffin cupped her cheek with his palm. "Maggie?"

"Hmmm."

"Tell me to kiss you." He leaned closer but resisted the urge to press his mouth to hers. "Please."

She stared into his eyes for several long seconds. "I'm not going to say that," she whispered after a moment.

Disappointment lashed at him, but when he started to pull away, she covered his hand with hers. "Remember what I told you about wanting to feel in control." She shifted so that only inches separated them, and her breasts grazed his shirtfront. "This is me taking control."

Then she kissed him.

Her lips were soft and she tasted like mint gum and Maggie. He'd missed this. Missed her.

Desire and emotion swirled through him, mingling so that it was difficult to know whether it was his body or his heart so overwhelmed by the moment.

He didn't wrap his arms around her or try to deepen the kiss. She was in control and her soft exploration was the most erotic thing he'd ever experienced.

Because it was Maggie. Because it gave him hope.

She made a sound, a barely audible hum of need but it seemed to break her out of the moment. She pulled back, her eyes clouded with desire, and raised a hand to her lips.

"I didn't mean that," she said, shaking her head.

He wanted to pull her to him, cover her mouth with his and prove that she not only meant it, but she wanted more. She wanted him, even if she wouldn't admit it.

He gave her what he hoped was a gentle smile. "I'll take it, just the same. Thank you." Before she could answer, argue with him or find a way to shore up the opening in the wall she'd erected around her heart, Griffin walked into the family room. He scooped up Joey, relieved when the boy's eyes remained closed.

"Call Andy Mason. He's the best plumber in town and an old friend of mine. If you need any more help, let me know."

She nodded, brushing the hair from Joey's forehead. "Thanks for coming over tonight. I hope the rest of it is peaceful."

"Good night, Maggie."

"Good night," she echoed, opening the front door to let them out.

The air was cold and smelled of snow. He walked to the SUV, a newfound hope making warmth spread across his chest. He wasn't giving up on her yet. Not by a long shot.

Chapter Seven

Saturday night, Maggie once again had a smile affixed to her face, only this time it was natural. She stood to one side of the sanctuary in the church where she'd once planned to be married, waiting for the audience to take their seats.

The Stonecreek Christmas Pageant was a holiday tradition that had been part of the town's busy December calendar since before Maggie was born. In fact, she'd played Mary twice, an unprecedented honor that her grandmother still reminded her of each Christmas season.

This year she had the responsibility of introducing the play since the event was being filmed for LiveSoft. She smiled at the kids who stood waiting behind the makeshift stage curtain they'd erected to one side of the pulpit. The group consisted of Mary,

Joseph, shepherds and the wise men and women plus various barn animals played by children ranging in age from six to eleven. A few years ago they'd tried to use real animals for the pageant, but one of the sheep had relieved itself in front of the altar, leading to general pandemonium and a whole lot of tears. The building custodian put a moratorium on animals after that fiasco.

But tonight would be perfect.

The sanctuary was standing room only. The pageant was universally loved in town. Whether or not people had a child or grandchild participating now, everyone crowded in to see the current production. There'd be talk for days over coffee and at the local hardware store about the delivery of lines and how cute Mary and Joseph had been together. At least a half dozen of the holy couples from years past had gone on to date in real life when they reached high school. Trevor had been Maggie's Joseph one year, although thankfully no one had reminded her of that recently.

Christian sat in the front row, sandwiched between his assistant Allyson on one side and Grammy on the other.

Griffin and Joey were behind them with Brenna and Marcus. Brenna's daughter Ellie was making her pageant debut as a lamb. Trevor sat a few pews away. Despite his betrayal during their relationship, she still considered him a friend. They'd spent a lot of these December evenings together over the years. She'd gone to coffee with him before he left for his trip and was glad to see him so happy at the prospect of his new venture.

Suzanne Bayer, the youth minister overseeing the pageant, gave Maggie her cue from the other side of the stage. Maggie walked out, shielding her eyes slightly as one of the student volunteers working the lights shone a spotlight directly on her face.

"Welcome," she said when she reached the microphone stand, "friends both old and new to Stonecreek and our annual Christmas pageant." She inclined her head toward Christian, who winked and flashed what felt like a suggestive smile at such a public event. Maggie cleared her throat, ignoring Griffin's narrowed eyes in the row behind the CEO. He couldn't possibly have seen how Christian looked at her.

"This is one of my favorite events of the season," she told the crowd. "In the craziness that often accompanies December, let's take an evening to remember what Christmas is really about. The kids have worked hard this year and they have a special performance planned for you. Without further ado, I give you our Nativity play."

She moved the stand to one side of the stage and lowered the microphone so that Lila Moore, the sixth grader who was narrating the pageant this year, could speak directly into it. As the girl spoke about the star of wonder appearing to the shepherds in the field, the kids in homemade robes tied with rope sashes filed onto the stage, along with a few floppy-eared donkeys and fluffy sheep.

Maggie watched from the shadows as the boy playing the star poked his head through the black curtain, only one star spoke getting stuck in the fabric. There was hushed laughter from the audience when a lamb sat back on his haunches and shoved a thumb in his mouth.

She glanced at the audience to see Christian watching the pageant with a look of bemused confusion on his face. It was almost as if he'd never seen children act before. He didn't seem bored, so that was one thing in their favor at least.

Maggie'd watched the footage from his most recent visit to their rival town Timmins. He'd had a difficult time feigning attention at the gingerbread house contest where he'd been an honorary judge.

Behind him, Griffin leaned down to whisper something to Joey, who smiled broadly. Maggie's heart stuttered as Griffin placed an arm around the boy's small shoulders. Then he looked up and met her gaze. Her breath caught at the emotion he allowed her to see in his green eyes.

She turned her attention back to the pageant as Lila described Mary and Joseph's journey and search for a place to stay with baby Jesus. The girl who was playing Mary, a tiny wisp of a thing with dark hair and big eyes made her entrance and the crowd applauded.

Mary was accompanied by a taller boy in the role of Joseph and another husky boy, who was acting as a donkey based on the floppy felt ears attached to the headband he wore and his gray sweatshirt and sweatpants. Someone had come up with the idea for Mary to ride in on the donkey so the kid with the ears was on all fours with the girl, who looked like she wanted to throw up from nerves, straddling his back, holding tight to the baby doll in her arms. At least they'd decided to forgo the actual birth of the baby and gone with a scenario where the Christ child had already been born as they traveled to the stable.

A hush fell over the audience as the trio made their procession across the stage. Even Maggie held her breath, wondering if the donkey was going to make it to the manger. The boy was quite a bit bigger than the girl playing Mary, but Maggie could see him wheezing for breath. Then a loud trumpeting noise broke the silence.

Maggie clasped a hand to her mouth. That couldn't have been—

"You farted on me," the donkey shouted, rearing up.

Mary tumbled from his back, smacking against the tile floor. "Did not," she yelled back, scrambling to her feet.

"Jessica. Braden." Mrs. Bayer leaned out from the other side of the church's nave. "Stay in your roles."

"She farted." Braden threw up his hands. "I *felt* it."

Laughter rang out from the audience and the other children let out a chorus of disgusted groans.

"Farting Mary," one of the shepherds called, holding his staff in front of him like a shield.

"Shut up," the girl, Jessica, hissed at the same time Mrs. Bayer hurried forward. But before she reached the pair, Jessica whacked Braden on the shoulder with the doll she held in her arms.

"She hit him with baby Jesus," a girl dressed as a goat—or maybe a cow—yelled.

"It's not baby Jesus," the teacher said. "It's my daughter's doll. Everyone stay calm." Her gaze darted to Maggie and she mouthed the words *help me*.

Right. Maggie needed to do something. Allyson

was still avidly videoing the whole fiasco as the rest of the audience seemed to look on with a mix of horror and fascination.

"Close the curtain," Maggie whispered to the volunteer standing behind her, then walked—with purpose she hoped—onto the stage. Suzanne Bayer was busy calming the donkey, who was furiously wiping at his back and complaining loudly about "fart juice."

Maggie took Mary's hand and lifted the doll out of her arms, doing her best to reswaddle it as she cradled the baby to her shoulder. She stepped closer to Lila, who was crying softly as she stared out at the crowd.

"It's going to be fine, girls," she murmured then bent toward the microphone. "We're going to take a short break due to some technical difficulties. Please sit tight for a few minutes and—" she ratcheted up her smile a few notches "—in the meantime, would anyone like to lead us in a few Christmas carols?"

The audience murmured amongst themselves, and there were a few guffaws of laughter from the high schoolers in the back row. When no one began to sing, an awkward silence descended.

"Anyone?" she asked. "Trust me. You don't want to hear me."

Her eyes darted to Griffin, and she felt color flood her cheeks as she remembered the first date they'd gone on where he'd gently teased her about her singing voice. As if reading her mind, his mouth lifted at one corner and a moment later he began humming the first few notes of "O Holy Night."

A few people turned to look at him, including

Christian and the LiveSoft assistant. Then he began to sing.

She knew his voice was amazing, but at the moment it sounded like Andrea Bocelli and Marvin Gaye had a vocal love child in Griffin. Maggie squeezed Jessica's hand when a few more people started singing. Maggie felt her shoulders relax ever so slightly as the entire audience seemed to join in the popular carol.

Her father, Morgan and Ben sang along, and Grammy looked vaguely pleased as she glanced around from her seat next to Christian.

Maggie tugged on Jessica's hand and led her and Lila off stage, where Mrs. Bayer was giving the other students a pep talk about the magic of Christmas and how the show must go on.

The woman flashed a grateful smile as Maggie approached. "Great thinking on the carol," she said. "Jessica, we're going to put everyone in their places around the manger."

The little girl shook her head. "I don't want to go back out." She sniffed. "It was an accident."

"Why don't you get everyone else in place," Maggie suggested to the harried youth minister. "I'd like to talk to Jessica for a minute. I think I understand a bit about what she's feeling."

Suzanne nodded and Maggie led the girl to a quiet corner.

"Have you ever farted on someone?" Jessica asked, swiping at her cheeks.

Maggie hid her smile. "No, but a few months ago I was really embarrassed in front of most of the town."

Jessica studied her for a long moment then nodded. "You were the runaway bride. My mom and grandma talked about you."

"Everyone did," Maggie agreed grimly. "It made me want to hide away forever."

"You aren't hiding now," Jessica said with a sniff.

"No, sweetie. I decided the best way to make people—myself included—forget about what happened was not to hide. As hard as it was, I held my chin high and went on with life." She smoothed the hair out of Jessica's face. "I think you can do the same thing with the Christmas pageant. Head over to the manger and be the best Mary this town has ever seen."

"Even better than you?"

"Way better than me." Maggie handed the doll to the girl.

Jessica held it tight to her chest. "Okay," she whispered.

Suzanne Bayer approached, giving Jessica an encouraging smile. "Is our Mary ready?"

The girl nodded and took her teacher's outstretched hand while Maggie breathed a sigh of relief.

"Thank you."

She turned as a frazzled-looking woman stepped out of the shadows.

"I'm Jessica's mom, Christine." Maggie shook the mom's outstretched hand. "She was so nervous about playing Mary anyway. I came back because my husband and I were sure she'd be in hysterics after what happened."

"She's handling it well." Maggie smiled. "Once she gets through the rest of the pageant, I hope she'll feel better."

"You helped. I thought it would upset her more to know I was here, and you did a great job of calming her. Thank you again."

"I've definitely been in her shoes." Maggie made a face. "Although not with…"

Christine chuckled. "I get it."

"Maggie," Suzanne called in a stage whisper. "We're ready to begin again."

"I'm going back to my seat," the mom said, "so I don't miss anything."

Maggie nodded and headed out into the spotlight. The audience finished the final chorus and fell quiet.

"Thanks for your patience," Maggie said into the microphone, gesturing for Lila to join her. "Let's continue with our story. Mary and Joseph arrived at the inn and found the only place available to house them is the stable. So the child has been placed in a manger and our lovely narrator is going to finish recounting the events of that night for you."

She backed away as the curtain opened. The crowd applauded loudly and one of the wise men waved to his parents. The rest of the pageant went off without a hitch, and the kids got a standing ovation at the end.

As soon as the play was finished, Maggie made her way through the crowd toward Christian and his assistant.

"That was quite a production," he said with a laugh.

"Yeah," she agreed. "About that." She looked between the two of them. "Any chance you could not post the first part of the pageant? I think people could get the spirit of the town just from the last bit and the kids taking their bow so—"

"Are you joking?" Allyson looked up from her phone. "I uploaded a snippet, and the video is already trending. 'Farting Mary.'" The woman, who couldn't have been more than a couple years younger than Maggie, gave a harsh laugh. "It's going to be an instant classic."

"It's going to embarrass an innocent girl," Maggie said firmly. "I'd like you to take it down." She moved closer to Allyson and tapped a finger on the top of her phone. "Now."

"Maggie, come on," Christian crooned. "You signed off on having us post content from our visits to Stonecreek. It's part of the contest."

"I understand," she said, keeping her features neutral. Most of the audience had dispersed but enough people still milled around the sanctuary that she didn't want to look like she was making a scene. Heaven forbid. "But this is different, Christian. It's personal to our community."

"Your community is part of a national promotion to become the location for LiveSoft's new headquarters," Allyson insisted. "Do you know how much tax revenue is on the line with this deal?"

"Yes," Maggie answered through clenched teeth. This woman had the heart of a grinch. "We're a small town. So I also know how embarrassing it could be for the girl to have the video splashed across social media. People in town will already be talking. I'm sure there are plenty of videos taken by parents in the audience. But public humiliation on a national stage is different than in a school auditorium."

"I'm sorry." Allyson shook her head. "But I won't—"

"Take it down," Christian interrupted, his gaze remaining on Maggie. "We don't need the footage."

"But it's hilarious," the assistant protested.

"That's not the point of the campaign."

Maggie breathed a sigh of relief. "Thank you so much."

"But," he continued, his blue eyes almost cunning, "we'll need something else to upload in place of the pageant."

"You can't use the second half from when the carols began? That was lovely, right?"

He gave a noncommittal shrug. "It might seem odd without the entrance of Mary and Joseph."

"Okay, it's down." Allyson looked up from her phone, adjusting her tortoiseshell glasses. "I can't control the previous views. But the content is no longer available from any account associated with LiveSoft."

"Thanks," Maggie said. "What do you think about using the later footage?"

Allyson nodded. "I should be able to—"

"It won't work," Christian insisted.

"Not at all," the assistant immediately agreed.

"I don't understand." Maggie clenched her fists at her sides. "Does this mean Stonecreek doesn't have anything to show for this week?"

"We can film something new tonight." Christian smoothed a hand over his shirtfront. "One of the things people are responding to is your success at attracting a younger, vibrant demographic to the town. It's a benefit for my employees, as well."

"I guess." At this point, Maggie was simply trying

to keep her head above water. But if he'd gotten the impression she'd been successful on any front, she wasn't about to disabuse him of that notion.

"You're the face of Stonecreek."

"Um…"

"I think we should use that to the town's advantage."

A frisson of unease slipped down her spine. "Um… use it how?"

"More focus on you."

She smiled and the familiar ache in her cheeks returned. "But the *focus* is the town. We want your employees to want to come here."

"You want *me* to want to come here," Christian countered. "Corporate relocations track closely with where the CEO lives. The board wants us in a smaller community, but I like my life in the city. I need a reason to relocate, if you know what I mean?"

"How about dinner and a carriage ride?" Allyson suggested cheerily. "We'll have the Christmas lights as a backdrop and can ask the store owners to stay open later. Maggie can give you a personal tour and really sell you on living here."

The words themselves were innocent, but somehow Allyson sounded like a bright-eyed and bushy-tailed pimp saying them.

Christian nodded. "Perfect. We've never had a chance for some time to ourselves."

"I'm n-not sure," Maggie stammered. "People are so busy this time of year. It's a lot to ask for shop owners to—"

"It's free publicity," Allyson said with an airy

laugh, suddenly as perky as Barbie after a double shot of espresso now that Christian seemed happy.

More like satisfied in the way of the cat that ate the canary, Maggie thought.

He tried to look innocent but Maggie could tell Christian Milken was a man who wanted to get his way in everything. Right now he wanted her. She'd managed to avoid going out with him up until this point and didn't appreciate being put on the spot now. She'd already had more than her fair share of notoriety in her personal life.

But the opportunity to house LiveSoft's headquarters was still the best chance she had to ensure Stonecreek's future. It was her chance to prove people had made the right choice in electing her.

To prove it to herself.

"It will be fun," Maggie said, refusing to admit, even to herself, how far she'd go to make sure Stonecreek won this competition. "Pick me up at six?"

"We'll be there," Allyson said then held up a hand when Christian frowned. "He'll be there. I mean, I'll be there to film, but I won't be part of the date because that would be weird and—"

"She gets the point," Christian said tightly. He turned so that he was blocking Allyson and placed his hands on Maggie's shoulders. "I'm looking forward to having an evening with just the two of us."

And all of LiveSoft's social media followers, Maggie wanted to add but smiled instead. "Me too."

He gently squeezed her shoulders, as if he were reluctant to let her go, but then turned and led Allyson out of the auditorium.

Maggie glanced around, thankful that the few

people still there seemed focused on cleaning up and breaking down the set. She left through a side door, needing time to collect herself before tonight.

Chapter Eight

"One other great thing about Stonecreek is you can see the stars at night." Maggie pointed to the sky above them then took a long sip of her hot chocolate, wishing Dora had laced the drink with a healthy swig of liquor. "You don't get that in the big city."

"Add it to the list," Christian said with the same winsome smile he'd been giving her all night. She wondered if his facial muscles ached as much as hers did. "It's clear you love this town."

"Yeah," she agreed, trying not to let her gaze dart to Allyson, who was snapping photos and taking videos every few minutes or whenever they entered a new shop.

Maggie had asked Brenna to call the business owners along Main Street and explain the idea for tonight. All of them had been happy to stay open and a couple had even enlisted "customers" to shop during their late hours.

Christian had been charming during dinner, peppering her with questions about her family and her interests outside her job. He was easy to talk to, although Maggie realized she still knew very little about him other than what she could find on his corporate bio. It seemed odd to have spent so much time with him in the last few weeks and still feel like he was a stranger.

She wondered how Griffin and Joey were doing? This morning her doorbell rang while she was still in her pajamas. A tiny part of her hoped he'd returned to check on her water but Andy the plumber had greeted her instead. He'd explained that Griffin had insisted he get to her house first thing to fix the pipe, even though he'd had emergency jobs already scheduled for the day.

"We have one more stop," she told Christian, trying her best to sound normal and not like this whole evening had been staged.

"Oh, drat." Allyson hopped down from the park bench she'd been standing on to film them as they walked along the sidewalk. "My phone is dead. Christian, can I use your camera and send everything to my phone to post?"

"I have a better idea," he answered, placing a hand on Maggie's back. "Let's take the rest of the night off from the competition."

Maggie noticed a split-second flash of disappointment in the other woman's eyes before she pocketed her phone and nodded. "Sure. I'm going to head back to the inn so…"

"Great. I'll see you tomorrow morning," Christian offered. "What time do we leave?"

"Nine," Allyson said quietly. "I'll have breakfast sent to your room at eight thirty. Two eggs over medium, just like you like them."

Christian was already turning to face Maggie. "Where to next?"

"Um…okay…" Allyson called with a limp wave. "Have a great rest of the night, you two."

"Do you want us to walk you to the hotel?" Maggie looked around Christian to smile at the assistant. "It's kind of late."

"I can't imagine any place safer than Stonecreek," Christian answered before Allyson could speak. "She'll be fine."

Maggie's stomach tightened as Allyson's mouth pressed into a thin line. Maggie had a suspicion the woman had a crush on her boss and didn't relish the idea of leaving Maggie alone with him. "I'm fine," the assistant repeated and quickly headed across the street.

She needed to find a way to communicate that she liked Christian as a friend but nothing more without offending him. She could tell him she didn't want a relationship, but it was only partly true.

As much as she tried to convince herself she was happier alone, her heart remained stubbornly fixated on Griffin. But she could ignore her heart. Easy-peasy.

"What are you thinking about?" Christian tipped his head to study her. "You look lost in thought."

"Toilets," she blurted then grimaced.

He chuckled. "A surprise answer. Good idea saving that revelation for off camera."

"Sorry. I need to stop by the hardware store and order a toilet for the bathroom I'm renovating. I keep forgetting to do it. I hope you don't mind the practical errand as part of your holiday tour of Stonecreek?"

"Not at all." She started to move forward but he quickly bent and brushed his lips across hers before falling into step next to her.

A sick feeling opened in the pit of her stomach as she glanced around to see if anyone had witnessed the kiss. Brief as it had been, tongues would be wagging all through town if word got out that LiveSoft's CEO had kissed her on the street.

"No reaction?" he asked, reaching down to take her hand as they walked.

She forced air in and out of her lungs. "That was a surprise, as well."

"I like you, Maggie." His voice had taken on a suggestive edge. "You have to know that."

"I like you, too, but we'd be crossing some boundaries we shouldn't if things got personal during the competition."

"Like I said earlier, the decision about a new headquarters *is* personal. I grew up on the East Coast. I'm used to big cities and nightlife. I understand why the board wants a change. A move to a smaller town for the new headquarters might be best for the company, but it's a stretch for me." His fingers tightened on hers. "I need to know I'm making the right choice."

A nervous laugh escaped her lips as she tugged her hand away under the guise of opening the door to Meyer's Hardware and Lumber. Certainly he wasn't insinuating that she should be that reason? Saying he liked her was a far cry from moving his entire company to a town because of her. Yes, she'd had concerns about his expectations, but part of her wanted to believe she was overreacting because of feedback from so many people in town. Now she wondered...

"Hey, Maggie," Kurt Meyer, the store's owner, called from the front counter. "What brings you in?"

"Toilets," she replied trying to muster another smile but finding it difficult.

"We have many fine types of bathroom fixtures at Meyer's Hardware and Lumber," Kurt continued, holding out his hands like he was giving a sermon. "As well as other tools and supplies a person new to town might need."

Maggie frowned. Kurt said the words in a staccato rhythm like he was a bad actor rehearsing lines for a play. And she'd lived in this town all her life. She wasn't new to Meyer's so why—

"Oh, Kurt, no." She waved her hands in front of her. "They're not taping right now. It's just Christian and me."

"Shopping for toilets," the CEO added drily.

Kurt wiped a hand across his brow and sighed. "What a relief. I've always had horrible stage fright. Worse than poor little Jessica tonight."

He leaned over the counter and touched a spot on the back of his head. "Feel this," he commanded.

"What the..." Christian muttered as Maggie stepped forward. Kurt had always been eccentric, but he was a decent person.

She reached out two fingers and rubbed them

against his scalp. The scent of wood shavings and Old Spice drifted toward her. "There's a bump."

He nodded, straightening. "I fell off the risers during our spring recital when I was in third grade. Passed out and knocked my head against the corner of the metal. I had a concussion and eight stitches. The bone never healed quite right."

"That explains a lot," Christian said under his breath as he joined Maggie at the counter.

She darted him a quelling look. She liked Kurt and wouldn't have anyone making fun of him.

"I'm sorry I didn't mention it right away." She patted the older man's rough hand. "We certainly don't want to stress you out. I forgot that everyone was staying open tonight for filming. I can stop in tomorrow during my lunch break."

Kurt waved away her concern. "Might as well look now. I'm here, and I'd much rather have you shopping than making me into some kind of Clark Gable wannabe."

"I bet you would have given him a run for his money back in the day."

A small snort from Christian had her glaring at him again.

"You're not my only customer, anyway," Kurt continued, oblivious to any judgment coming from the man next to her. "I might need to extend my hours on a regular basis."

"Although I'm not in the market for something as exciting as a new toilet," a deep voice said from down one of the aisles.

Griffin appeared at the endcap, wearing a thick down jacket over a dark sweater and jeans.

"Hey, man." Christian immediately moved forward, shaking Griffin's hand enthusiastically. "What are you doing here?"

"Great question," Maggie added, lifting a brow even as butterflies flitted across her stomach. The last thing she needed adding another complication to this night was Griffin, although she couldn't deny how happy she was to see him.

Griffin smiled as the CEO shook his hand. Christian's palm felt as smooth as a baby's bottom, another mark against him as far as Griffin was concerned. "Brenna called and said they were looking for extras for filming tonight. I needed a few things from here, anyway, so it will save me a trip into town tomorrow."

"Don't tell me that a trip to the hardware store is the most excitement this town has to offer on a Saturday night," Christian said with a groan. "Throw me a bone."

"You should grab a drink at O'Malley's across the street," Griffin answered, faking enthusiasm. "Chuck pulls in a decent crowd."

He knew Maggie had spent the evening with Christian. Hell, it was the reason Griffin had agreed to an after-hours trip into town. As far as he could tell, the whole town was buzzing about Maggie going on a date with the CEO. He wanted to believe she was doing it for the competition but had to see for himself.

He glanced over at her now, and his heart squeezed when she gave him a quick, private smile.

"Yeah," Kurt agreed from behind the counter. "And they've got karaoke on Thursday nights with a professional machine. Irma Cole can belt out Lady Gaga like nobody's business."

"Fantastic," Christian said with an eye roll.

"It's fun." Maggie stepped forward, placing a hand on the other man's arm. Griffin felt his eyes narrow. "We should all go sometime."

"Um…okay." Griffin had never known Maggie to show up for karaoke night and he sure as hell wasn't planning on—

"You probably heard Griffin leading the carol tonight," she continued. "He has a great voice. Thanks for that, by the way." Pink colored her cheeks. "It helped keep everyone calm while we figured things out backstage."

"Sure." He tipped his head to study her, trying to figure out what was wrong. Her eyes were too bright and one of her hands was clenched in a tight fist, pressing against her stomach.

"Right now I could use a drink," Christian announced. He draped an arm over Maggie's shoulder, winding his fingers through the ends of her long hair. "Maggie, do you mind holding off on the bathroom shopping until tomorrow? I'd like to get out of here."

She shifted away slightly, but when the other man didn't let go seemed to settle into the embrace. "That's fine." She glanced over her shoulder. "Kurt, I'll stop by in the morning."

The older man held up a hand. "I'll plan on having a bran muffin for breakfast so I'm ready to talk toilets." He laughed at his own potty-humor joke. "If you know what I mean?"

"Unfortunately, I do," Maggie answered with a nod.

"You want to join us?" Christian asked, but Griffin shook his head, not trusting himself to speak when the guy was hanging on to Maggie like she belonged to him. "Fine then. I'll give you a call when I'm coming to town next. I'd like to talk more about the sustainability of your new tasting room construction. If LiveSoft ends up in Stonecreek, the board is going to want to implement some of those initiatives in building the headquarters."

"Fine then." Griffin echoed Christian's words when it was clear he had to say something.

He turned without saying goodbye to Maggie and headed back down the aisle to pick up a new blade for his miter saw. Kurt didn't seem like he was in any hurry to lock up for the night, so Griffin took his time. There was no way he wanted to take a chance on running into Maggie and Christian walking through town arm in arm.

By the time he got to the counter, snow fell outside the window, coming down in thick, heavy flakes that almost created a whiteout effect.

"Mind if I come back in the morning for the wood?"

Kurt glanced from the flatbed cart stacked with boards then behind him at the sudden storm. "No problem." He used the scanner to ring up Griffin's purchase. "Maggie's doing us a solid, you know?"

"Know what?" Griffin tapped an impatient finger on the counter.

"That CEO guy is obviously smitten and she's going above and beyond to make sure he's happy in Stonecreek."

He had no interest in knowing what Kurt meant by "above and beyond."

"The town can sell itself. If the company picks Stonecreek, great. If not, we'll be fine."

Kurt shrugged. "The tax money would go a long way around here."

Griffin waited while Kurt bagged his purchases, trying not to think of Maggie and Christian together—and failing miserably.

"I guess we'll see what happens in a few weeks. Have a good night, Kurt. Enjoy your muffin tomorrow."

"The wife puts extra raisins in them," Kurt said, because that's how I like it.

"You're a lucky guy." With a final wave, Griffin left the store and was immediately covered in snow. The flakes were fluffy and cold on his heated skin, and he could almost hear them sizzle as they landed. It had been a stupid idea to come to town tonight. Maggie made it clear she'd accept his friendship and nothing more. Now he had an ill sensation in his gut to accompany him on the way back to the vineyard. His car was parked around the corner. As he approached, he saw the outline of a woman sitting on his back bumper.

Maggie.

Her head was bent forward, her hands folded in her lap. A dusting of white snow covered her, giving her almost an ethereal quality. He guessed she'd been there at least five minutes.

The streets were empty as most of the town would be home at this hour. Unless there was an event, Stonecreek rolled up the sidewalks early.

So why was Maggie here waiting for him?

His boots crunched in the wet snow as he approached, but she didn't look up. There was something about a heavy snowfall that made the world close in on itself. It felt like they were the only two people for miles. The air was already cold, and he could feel the temperature dropping quickly.

"Hey," he said when he was directly in front of her. Her eyes remained closed, dark lashes resting against her pale skin. Griffin crouched down in front of her, dropping his bag to the ground and covering her hands with his. "Maggie, what's going on?"

Her fingers were like ice, and he suddenly realized she was shivering madly. He brushed the snow out of her lap and off her shoulders as she blinked and focused her gaze on him, seeming almost surprised to find him in front of her.

"You're freezing," he said, pulling her to her feet. "Let's get in the car."

"I'm messing it all up." She let herself be led to the passenger side of the Land Cruiser. He unlocked the door and she climbed in.

"I want to hear everything," he promised. "But we need to reheat you first."

He plucked the bag off the ground then got into the car, placing his purchases in the backseat. Turning the key in the ignition, he prayed for the heat to kick in quickly as he adjusted the vents to aim at Maggie.

"I'm going to take you home," he told her, already pulling onto the street. "I don't know what's going on but you're in no shape to drive in this weather. We can pick up your car wherever it's parked tomorrow."

She shook her head. "Chr-christian picked m-me up," she said through chattering teeth.

"The date," he muttered. "I heard. Where is he

now?" He glanced at her huddled in the seat next to him and then cursed when he felt the vents, which were still blowing cool air. "Why didn't he take you home?"

"H-he wanted me t-to come to h-his hotel," she said and Griffin wished he could transfer some of the heat raging through his body to hers.

"I'll kill him," he whispered automatically.

She shook her head. "N-not for that. A d-drink. That's all."

Right. Griffin could only imagine how the amorous CEO wanted only to share a nightcap with Maggie. In his hotel room. Because that's just how powerful men worked.

Luckily Maggie lived in the neighborhood adjacent to downtown, and he was pulling into her driveway within minutes.

As he came around the front of the car, she started to climb out. He scooped her into his arms and slammed shut the door, stalking toward the house.

Maggie laughed into his coat. "Th-this is like m-my wedding d-day. I c-can walk."

"I'm well aware," he said under his breath but didn't put her down until they were on the front porch. In truth, it was difficult to force himself to release her even then.

Yes, he'd carried her to her house after she'd twisted her ankle fleeing from the church and her impending marriage to his brother. But six months ago felt like a lifetime in the past. At that point, he'd felt sorry for Maggie. Before he'd even known the details, it was clear Trevor had hurt her. He'd appreciated her spunk and the way she'd tried to be brave but now...

Now he loved her.

Something about her interaction with Christian Milken tonight had forced her out into a snowstorm and clearly messed with her head.

Truly, he was going to destroy the man, if not literally then he'd find a way to wreck him for hurting Maggie.

No one hurt Maggie.

He inwardly cringed as he watched her struggle to unlock the front door with trembling fingers. The only thing that stopped him from taking the key from her was the knowledge that he'd hurt her—probably far worse than whatever Christian had done.

Griffin should see her safely inside then leave. She was stronger than she realized. He had no doubt she'd find a way to make right whatever it was she thought she'd "messed up."

But he wouldn't leave. He couldn't.

The door clicked open and he followed her in, watching as she flipped on lights and cupped her hands in front of her mouth to breathe warm air onto them.

"You should get out of those clothes."

She gave him a dubious look. "And you're upset about Christian asking me for a drink?"

"Into something warm and dry," he clarified. "I'll heat water for tea."

She studied him a moment longer then sighed. "Thank you."

He ran a hand through his hair as he watched her disappear up the stairs. On the way to the kitchen, he texted his mom to tell her something had happened with Maggie and he might not be home until later. She confirmed that Joey was sleeping soundly and that she could handle things if the boy woke.

For years, Griffin had prided himself on the fact that he didn't have messy attachments to people. Any attachments, really. He'd been estranged from his family and although he would have done anything for his army buddies, now he felt completely enmeshed in the lives of the people he cared about. Downright domesticated if he faced the truth.

It suited him, much to his surprise.

He heated water on the stove and opened cabinets until he found a container of chamomile tea bags. He dropped one into a mug and waited for the kettle to whistle.

A few pieces of sample tile and paint swatches were spread across the counter. Maggie was taking control of her life, and pride flooded him at her determination.

That determination filled her gray eyes as she walked into the room wearing a thick fleece pullover and black yoga pants. Were yoga pants supposed to be sexy? Probably not, but the fact that he found them seriously arousing said a lot about his state of mind at the moment.

"Thank you for getting me home tonight," she said, her tone crisp. "I overreacted."

"To Christian putting the moves on you?" He shook his head. "I doubt it."

A keening whistle sounded from the teapot and he flipped off the burner then poured steaming water into a mug.

"You aren't joining me?" she asked, stepping closer.

"Tea isn't really my thing."

"A beer?"

"If you have one."

She opened the refrigerator and pulled out a bottle. He dunked the tea bag several times then they traded—tea for her and a microbrew for him.

"You could lace it with whiskey," he suggested as he lifted the bottle to his lips.

She smiled and shook her head. "I had wine with dinner. I'm kind of a lightweight."

"Only when it comes to alcohol," he reminded her.

She sipped the tea, spreading her fingers around the mug. "This is perfect. I thought I'd never be warm again. Probably not in the best interest of the town if I let myself freeze before the competition is over."

"The town will be fine." He repeated his earlier words to Kurt then held up a hand when her eyes widened. "Without LiveSoft," he clarified. "Not you. We need you."

"I appreciate that, especially after tonight."

His grip tightened on the beer bottle. "What happened with Christian?"

"Nothing." She bit down on her lower lip. "Yet."

"Remember when I punched Trevor in the sanctuary after you walked away from the wedding?"

She nodded and rolled her eyes. "I don't need—"

"If I decked that sanctimonious CEO," he interrupted, "it would be as much for me as for you. That guy rubs me the wrong way."

"He likes me," she blurted.

"He's human," he countered, earning another eye roll.

"It's going to mess up everything. He basically told me that I'd be his biggest reason for choosing Stonecreek as the headquarters."

"I thought the social media followers voted and the board makes the final decision."

"Well, yes, but Christian's assistant edits all of the content. She directs the narrative, and apparently they want me to be part of it."

"What do you want?" he forced himself to ask.

"To take care of the town."

"By dating our potential rainmaker?"

"I don't want to date Christian," she insisted with more conviction than he would have expected after she'd spent the evening with the guy.

"But you went out with him tonight."

She set the mug onto the counter then pressed her palm against her forehead. "I asked them to delete the footage of Jessica's embarrassing moment at the pageant."

"Good for you."

"He suggested I go to dinner with him in return— just the two of us. Well, the two of us and a camera. They needed replacement content." She shook her head. "Brenna called everyone about staying open late. I thought it would be an easy way to get additional publicity for some of the local businesses."

"The town is doing great on its own."

"There are still struggles. Budget constraints that most people don't see. With an influx of tax revenue, I could do so much. The community deserves more. Everyone thinks we're going to win the competition."

"We could," he said quietly.

"Christian needs an incentive to give up the big city for small-town life."

"How is it that you don't want me to kill him?"

"I want to believe he means it as a compliment."

"Maggie, come on."

"Okay," she said, throwing up her hands. "But I can't be rude about it."

"Hell, yeah, you can."

"I'll mess up our chances," she protested.

"It doesn't matter."

"You don't understand."

"I understand that you aren't going to be bullied into dating or whatever else with some powerful corporate honcho to win. You aren't part of the bargain. Not even your grandmother would expect that."

She gave a small laugh. "Have you met her?"

He placed the beer on the counter and moved closer, reaching out a hand to cup her cheek. "How can I help?"

She stared up at him as if seeing him for the first time.

Damn, he hoped that was true. He wanted her to see him for the man he could become. The kind of guy who deserved to be a part of her life.

Chapter Nine

Who was this man standing in front of her?

Maggie leaned into Griffin's touch, loving the warmth of his hand. Yes, he'd hurt her but he'd also been a consistent support in these past few months. Every time she needed him or asked him for anything, he made himself available.

It was more than physical attraction, although wanting him remained a palpable force in her life. He was a friend, maybe the best friend she had.

"I want to make this town look so good that LiveSoft will have no choice but to pick Stonecreek. I'm not sure exactly how to do that…how to add anything more than what we've already got."

"He's interested in spending more time at the vineyard. To be honest, I've been blowing him off since the last meeting because I'm already so busy getting up to speed with everything before Marcus leaves and adding Joey into the mix."

"How are things with him?"

Griffin's handsome features didn't change, but she could feel the tension in him as he thought about the boy. "It changes on a daily, and sometimes hourly, basis. I guess that's normal for kids in general, and especially with what he's been through."

"Yes," she agreed.

"Parenting is damn hard."

She smiled. "A universal truth."

"It doesn't help that he has to face Christmas so soon after his mom died. He actually really enjoyed the pageant tonight, and not just because of Mary and the donkey. I'm trying to figure out how Cassie handled the holidays and honor the traditions he already knows. But my mom has her own way of doing things too. We tried to decorate the tree last night and Joey threw a fit because it's artificial."

"A fit? Surely you're exaggerating."

He shook his head. "Apparently Cassie had something against artificial trees. I don't get it but he insisted it's not Christmas without a real tree."

"What did your mom say?"

"She told me to get a real tree and we'd wait to decorate until then."

"She's the best."

"Absolutely," Griffin agreed.

"My problems aren't your problem," she reminded him. "You have plenty to deal with right now."

He touched one finger to her lips, gently silencing her. "I want to help. I'll invite Christian back out to the vineyard and make it clear that everyone at Harvest is committed to helping his company transition into the community."

"That would be great," she said, reaching out to spread her hand over his chest. She could feel his heart beating, strong and steady under his shirt.

"I don't want you stressed out by all this," he murmured, running the pad of his thumb across her cheek.

She laughed softly. "Too late."

"You are smart, dedicated and amazing with what you do for this town. No one doubts that."

"I want to win," she told him honestly. "So much."

"Then we'll make sure you do," he promised.

She pulled away and gripped his arm, making a show of looking over his shoulder.

"What's that about?"

"Just checking to see if your hero cape is showing."

"Nah. Costumes aren't really my thing."

"Too bad," she said, tapping a finger on his chin. "I had a couple of superhero fantasies I was hoping to explore."

"Always killing me," he muttered as his eyes went dark with desire.

She wound her arms around his neck. Suddenly the past didn't matter. The pain she'd felt disappeared. In its place, sensual sensation sparked along her skin.

He kissed her, deep and hungry. Maggie loved his mouth, the way it was soft and smooth, a contrast to his stubbled jaw and the hard planes of his body.

She'd missed kissing him, missed being close to him in a way that made this moment all the more precious.

Desire and need flowed through her veins, co-
alescing at her aroused center. Griffin's hands snaked
up between their bodies, skimming under her shirt.
She grabbed the hem and lifted it over her head.

"No bra," he murmured with a wicked smile. "I
approve."

"No panties either," she told him, her voice raspy
with need.

"You've moved past superhero status," he said,
tugging on her waistband. "You're a goddess."

She laughed and stepped out of her yoga pants.
She'd missed this too—how easy it was to laugh with
him when they were together. Maggie wasn't exactly
known for her playfulness, but Griffin had a way of
making everything more fun. "*You're* overdressed."

"Easily remedied," he said as he toed off his boots.
She watched his rapid striptease with a wide smile,
her breath catching at the sight of his taut muscles.

But when he reached for her, she held up a hand.
"We're in my kitchen."

He made a show of glancing around. "So we are.
Is that a problem?"

"Um…not exactly…but…"

"I think we can make it work," he promised, pulling her into his arms.

No sooner had she nodded her agreement than he
gripped her waist and placed her on the table. His hands
slid from her hips, down her thighs until he reached
her knees, gently nudging them apart. He touched her
exactly where and how she longed to be touched, and
she moaned with need.

At the same time, he claimed her mouth again,
his tongue mimicking the movements of his fingers.

Within minutes she'd lost herself in the sensations assaulting her, tiny pinpricks of pleasure cascading through her body. The pressure built until her pounding desire drowned out every doubt she'd had about Griffin.

She tried to remind herself that this was only physical. It couldn't mean what she wanted it to, but her body and heart refused to cooperate.

Then he pulled away and she whimpered a protest, wondering if he'd somehow been able to sense her internal struggle.

She was left gasping for breath, balanced on her elbows as he bent toward his discarded jeans.

A moment later he straightened, holding a silver packet. "I need to be inside you," he said, giving her a lopsided smile. "I can't wait, Maggie."

Tugging her bottom lip between her teeth, she nodded. Her lady parts gave a cheer of delight while the doubts she knew would eventually resurface disappeared into the dark recesses of her heart.

Griffin braced a hand on the table and she held on to his shoulders as he pressed forward and entered her.

It was like finding a piece of herself that had been missing.

He moved, shifting his grip on her to anchor her hips. She wound her legs around his waist and arched into him, relishing his strength and control with each powerful thrust.

Tension tightened her belly, and Griffin grazed his lips over her sensitive earlobe. "Let go," he commanded, and she did, spiraling over the edge of desire without any thought to landing on the other side.

But Griffin was there, holding her tight, groaning his own release into the crook of her neck. She felt limp and boneless, and he continued to cradle her in his arms like she was something precious.

"I'll never look at a bowl of cereal the same way again," she whispered when her breathing had almost returned to normal.

He chuckled and pulled back, only to pick her up and carry her to her bedroom.

"Can you stay?" she asked, too content to worry about the need that threaded through her voice.

"For a while," he whispered and kissed the tip of her nose.

She smiled and welcomed him into her bed, still forcing herself to remain focused on this moment and nothing more.

"What if we get lost?" Joey asked from the backseat of Griffin's Land Cruiser the following morning.

"I promise we won't get lost," Griffin said, glancing at the boy in the rearview mirror.

"Don't they sell Christmas trees here in parking lots like normal?"

Maggie laughed and turned in her seat. "Joey, I promise we're going to find the best tree ever this way. One for my house and one for yours. I appreciate both of you joining me for this little outing. I haven't cut down a tree in the woods since I was a girl."

"I think Miss Jana was sad to put away her fake tree," Joey observed, his brown eyes solemn. "But Mommy said fake trees were boring."

Maggie saw Griffin grimace. "Miss Jana wants

you to have a great Christmas. If it makes you happy to have a real tree, she'll be happy."

The boy nodded and continued tracing shapes in the condensation on the back window.

As Griffin left late last night, Maggie'd impulsively suggested they take Joey on an outing for a Christmas tree today. Her thoughts had been in sync with Joey's—a quick trip to the local garden center, where they shipped in trees from Washington State. But this morning Griffin had texted to ask if she'd be up for a hike in the woods and cutting down their own trees. He thought it would be something new and different for Joey without having to compare it to how Cassie had handled the tradition.

New traditions. 'Twas the season for that it seemed.

With last night's heavy snow, the drive was slow out of town and into the nearby Strouds Run State Park. Griffin had borrowed one of the vineyard's extended cab pickups so it would be easy to load the trees into the back.

They parked at the trailhead and climbed out. The sky was clear, the air crisp and scented with pine. Maggie pulled three packets of hand warmers from her purse.

"Let's drop these into your mittens," she told Joey, crouching down in front of the boy while Griffin collected a hand saw and ropes from the truck bed. "They'll keep your fingers toasty warm."

"Cool," he whispered, still sounding dubious about their impending adventure in the woods. He gave her the mittens and she slipped a warmer into each one of them then helped him put them on. The boy was adorable bundled up in a thick winter jacket, a wool hat with earflaps and a matching scarf.

"It's going to be fun," she promised, glancing around the frozen forest that surrounded them as she tightened his scarf.

He wrapped his arms around her, giving her a sweet if unexpected hug.

She blinked away sudden tears, overwhelmed that this sweet boy seemed to be trying to comfort her in the same way she was for him.

"Maggie has warmers for your hands," Joey announced to Griffin when he joined them.

"I'll be fine," he said gently. "I appreciate the thought though."

Maggie turned away for a moment to swipe at her eyes.

"It's those little moments that get you," Griffin said under his breath as Joey ran forward to touch an icicle hanging from a tree branch.

"I wasn't expecting it," she admitted. "It makes me think of all the hugs he'll miss giving his mom. All the hugs Morgan and Ben missed."

"Yeah," Griffin breathed. "But they had you. Thanks for being part of this day with us. It means a lot."

She drew in a breath then smiled as she shoved the hand warmers into her own mittens. "I'm not freezing my fingers."

"Don't worry." Griffin stepped closer. "I'll warm you if you need it later."

Heat swirled through her at the intimacy in his tone. "I'll remember that."

They started into the woods, with Joey leading the

way. The overnight snowfall, practically a record in Stonecreek, had left about four inches on the ground, so they moved slowly, which was fine with Maggie. She was grateful to be away from town and all the doubts and worries about the competition swirling through her mind.

The trees were thick in this part of the woods, which was why the parks department issued licenses for the trees. With snow weighing down the branches and sunlight making the crystals sparkle like diamonds, it was like walking through an actual winter wonderland.

"Let me know when you find the perfect tree," Griffin called to the boy.

Joey nodded but continued trudging through the ankle-deep snow. Every few feet he'd reach out a hand to touch one of the low-hanging branches, as if he could feel which tree to choose.

About two hundred yards in he stopped. "This one," he said, pointing to a tree that was not much bigger than a shrub.

"It's kind of small," Griffin said slowly, darting a help-me look toward Maggie.

"As I remember it, Miss Jana has a lot of ornaments to hang on the tree. You might want to look for one that's a tiny bit taller."

Joey wiped his nose with one mitten. "This tree needs us." He raised his arms to indicate the huge pines that surrounded the scraggly pine he'd chosen. "All the other ones are so big that he can't get enough sun. He's not happy being the littlest guy with no friends around. We have to take him so he's not alone for Christmas."

Maggie fluttered her mittens in front of her eyes as tears sprang to them once again. The small tree was indeed receiving only thin shafts of sunlight, even though it was a particularly bright day for Oregon in December.

"I'm going to need to invest in waterproof mascara if I ever have kids," she mumbled. "Who knew I was such a crier?"

Griffin wrapped an arm around her shoulder and pulled her close, kissing the top of her head. "You'll be a great mom." He grinned at the boy. "Your logic makes total sense. Miss Jana has been talking about simplifying her life for years. I think a great place to start is by downsizing her Christmas decorations."

"What's downsizing?" Joey asked as he brushed snow off the tiny tree's branches.

"Getting rid of the stuff you don't need anymore."

"Mommy got rid of all her stuff after she called you to come to Seattle. 'Cause she wouldn't need it in heaven."

Maggie leaned her head on Griffin's shoulder, unsure how her heart would make it through this outing.

"Your mommy took care of things," Griffin confirmed. "I bet it would make her very happy that you chose this tree." With a squeeze to Maggie's shoulder, he stepped forward with his saw. "Plus this little guy will be easy to get back to the truck. Well done, Joey. Well done."

The boy's face lit with pride. "What can I do to help?"

Griffin gave him instructions for helping then knelt in the snow and began sawing the base of the trunk. Because the tree was small, it came down in minutes.

"Hey, Freddie," Joey said, patting one of the branches as if greeting an old friend.

"You're naming it?"

"All living things have a spirit. The tree's spirit is named Freddie."

Maggie expected Griffin to scoff or tell the boy he was being ridiculous. Instead, he straightened, then lifted the tree and set it against the trunk of another larger pine. "Say goodbye to your neighbors, Freddie." He spoke directly to the tree then inclined his head like he was listening to an answer. "That's right. You're the best tree in the forest so you're coming home for Christmas." He paused again then turned to Joey. "Freddie says thank you."

Joey giggled and shook his head. "Trees can't talk."

"His spirit talked to me," Griffin explained.

Joey thought about that for a moment then nodded. "You're welcome," he told the tree.

Griffin winked at Maggie and his smile was so filled with tenderness that her heart melted as fast as a snowball held over an open flame. How had she ever thought she could keep this man out of her life forever?

The pain that had seemed to consume her felt like a lifetime ago, and she couldn't help but believe he'd truly changed since becoming the boy's guardian. It had only been a matter of weeks but he was different than he'd been before, grounded in a way she could never have imagined.

It was deeply appealing, and she could almost feel

her ovaries doing a little happy dance of solidarity. Oh, yes. Every part of Maggie appreciated the new and improved Griffin Stone.

Every cell in her body wanted him.

And her whole, recently patched-up heart loved him.

She was in trouble. Big time.

"We need to find a tree for you." Joey tugged on her sleeve. "Do you want a big one or small?"

She swallowed back the emotions bubbling up inside her and tried to make her voice normal. "How about one that's just the right size?"

"You should get a girl," the boy said, slipping his hand into hers. "Freddie kind of wants a girlfriend."

"Freddie's a little young to be thinking about girls," Maggie answered, squeezing his fingers gently.

They continued through the forest, the boy telling her about the different friends he'd had at his daycare center in Seattle. He explained that Bennie liked race cars, Dante loved dinosaurs and Julian wasn't good at sharing his toys.

"But Emma was my best friend," Joey shared. "Her mommy and daddy got divorced. It's not the same as dying but they don't live together anymore, and she doesn't get to see her daddy very much. I gave her a hug when she was sad."

"She was lucky to have a friend like you." Maggie glanced over her shoulder to find Griffin following them with an incredulous grin on his face.

"I'm going to start preschool after Christmas." Joey wiped his nose again. "Miss Jana said I can pick out a brand-new backpack, even though I already have one with trucks on it. I'm gonna get purple camo this time. Purple's my favorite color."

"Mine too," Maggie told him.

"What's your favorite color, Griffin?" the boy called.

"Blue," Griffin answered.

"That was Mommy's favorite. She wanted to get a puppy and name it Blue."

"Is that so?" Maggie asked but before she could warn him about how much work a puppy would take, Joey let out a small squeal.

"There it is," he called. "It's Freddie's friend."

He kicked up snow as he ran and then stopped in front of a pint-size tree that looked just as pathetic as the one he'd chosen for himself. "Do you love her?" he asked, beginning to brush snow from the branches.

"I hope he's directing that question at me," Griffin said from directly behind Maggie. She whirled around, her cheek brushing the collar of his coat. The way he was looking at her left her breathless as warmth flooded her body.

"He's talking about the tree," she said, pushing at his chest. It was like trying to move a slab of granite. She turned back toward the boy, trying her best to ignore Griffin and the way her body reacted to his nearness. So much trouble.

"I do love the tree," she told Joey. "What do you think we should name her?"

"Fiona," he answered after a moment. "Freddie and Fiona will be best friends like me and Emma."

"You're my best friend," Griffin told her, his

breath tickling her ear. "I don't know how I ever got through life without you."

"You shouldn't say things like that," she admonished, even as her heart skipped a beat.

"But it's the truth." He leaned in and kissed her cheek, the spicy, minty scent of him doing crazy things to her senses. "You're some kind of miracle worker with Joey. I haven't ever heard him talk so much. He sounds happy."

"He is," she assured him. "Or at least he will be again. We have to believe that."

She glanced at the boy, who was having a sincere conversation with the pine tree then turned to face Griffin, lifting a mittened hand to his cheek. "He's been through something terrible, but he has you. It sounds like Cassie was a great mom, so he also has a foundation of love in his life. It won't be easy, but I have faith in you to see him through."

Griffin sucked in a deep breath as he studied her face. "Thank you," he whispered, his eyes crinkling at the corners the way they did when he was truly happy. "This is the first time I've believed that since this whole thing started."

"Griffin, can we cut her down now?" Joey asked, his eyes dancing with delight. "I want to bring her over to Freddie."

"We sure can, buddy." Griffin stepped forward. "After we make the big introduction and load them into the back of the SUV, how about we stop for hot chocolate and a cookie in town?"

"Yes," Joey answered immediately, pumping his fist in the air. "Can Maggie come?"

Griffin raised an eyebrow in her direction then

gave a pretty decent imitation of a courtly bow—at least in Maggie's opinion. "Ms. Spencer, would you care to join Master Joey and I post–tree cutting as we raise a hot chocolate mug in celebration of the honorable Freddie and Fiona?"

She laughed despite her immediate reservation. It would certainly set the gossips on a tear if she was seen with Griffin and his new charge in town. Especially on the night after everyone knew she'd been out to dinner with Christian.

As Griffin studied her face, his smile faded. "If not—"

"Of course I'd love to," she answered. "But only if you promise we can get extra whipped cream."

Joey clapped his hands and Griffin's gaze seemed to soften once again. "As much whipped cream as you can handle."

Chapter Ten

Jana studied her reflection in the mirror above the foyer table that afternoon. The house was empty and the sunlight streaming in from the picture window in the adjacent living room seemed to highlight every one of her wrinkles and laugh lines. She practiced a smile then groaned at the crow's feet fanning out from the edges of her eyes.

Never before had she so appreciated the old adage that youth is wasted on the young.

As a car engine sounded from the drive, she slicked on a coat of lip gloss, furtively wiped at her mouth with the back of her hand then quickly re-applied the subtle shade. It was silly that she wanted to look her best for an outing to the foundry Jim used to cast his sculptures.

She hadn't seen him since the kiss they'd shared in

his studio the previous week, although they'd spoken several times to discuss her ideas for the sculpture. To her surprise, each phone call had lasted close to an hour. She felt like a teenage girl again, sitting on the edge of her bed with butterflies flitting across her stomach as she discussed everything and nothing with the boy she secretly liked.

If Griffin or Marcus noted her preoccupation, neither of them mentioned it. She guessed they were too busy with their own schedules to pay any attention to her. That was the amazing thing about reconnecting with Jim. For the first time in years—maybe decades—Jana felt like someone truly noticed her.

Her marriage to Dave Stone had been mainly a happy one, other than his rift with Griffin. But the vines had driven her husband, made him restless in a way she couldn't seem to satisfy. Although she'd never confirmed it, she was almost certain he'd cheated on her. In their later years together, the marriage was much more a platonic partnership rather than any bit of a love affair.

Jana had been satisfied, or at least she thought she had. Something new was unfurling inside her. She didn't believe in regrets, yet life seemed to be giving her the do-over she hadn't even realized she wanted.

She opened the front door just as Jim started up the steps. "You didn't have to—" She stopped, her gaze catching on the bouquet of red roses and stargazer lilies he held.

"These are for you," he said with an almost bashful smile.

"Oh," she breathed, reaching out a hand to take the lovely blooms from him.

"I had to stop at the hardware store on my way here. These were in the window of the florist. The colors looked so bright against the snow." He shrugged. "It's probably silly, but I thought you'd like them."

"I do," she said, breathing in the sweet scent. "Thank you." She held out the bouquet, which did look especially colorful in contrast with the snow that was just starting to melt. The temperature had risen to almost twenty degrees today, though still nowhere near normal in Stonecreek during December. They rarely got more than a dusting of snow in this part of the state. The unexpected storm made for a festive backdrop the week before Christmas, but the monochromatic color scheme it created was unusual. The flowers were a welcome pop of color.

"Please come in for a minute while I put them in water."

She led him into the house, realizing that this was probably the first time he'd ever been in her home. The house she'd shared with her husband. Although other than her visit to the studio, she'd never been in Jim's house. She could imagine it though—eclectic and a bit cluttered, classic without taking itself too seriously. A lot like the man himself.

"You have a beautiful home," he said, as if reading her thoughts.

She glanced over her shoulder and smiled. "It's only in the past few years that I felt like it belonged to me."

"I thought you and Dave lived here for years."

"We did, but his mother was alive for most of that time. She died only six months before him. Mrs.

Stone had strong views on the decor of her home. Quite strong."

He chuckled. "Even though she no longer lived here?"

She pulled a vase from an upper cabinet. "I imagine Vivian would feel the same way."

"You're right," he admitted. "In fact, Maggie is starting to renovate the old house and it's driving Mom absolutely crazy. She keeps lecturing her on respecting the past, and the quality of workmanship and materials in the good old days." He shrugged. "The problem is she can't give up control."

"No offense to your mother, but Charlotte must have been a saint to deal with her. I can't imagine Vivian making it easy for anyone."

One big shoulder lifted again then dropped. "We managed, but I let my mother have too much influence when I was younger. I'm not proud of that."

Her fingers trembled as she unwrapped the flowers and pulled scissors from a drawer to trim the stems. Of course he was talking about her. About the year they'd dated and how his mother had deemed Jana's blue-collar background inferior for her beloved son. It was old news now. Vivian had to give Jana and all the Stones the respect they deserved, even if it was grudging.

Jana had more than earned her place in this community. Why did it still sting that the first boy she'd given her heart to hadn't fought for her?

"We all make mistakes," she said, and they both ignored the false cheer in her voice.

She turned to the sink and filled the vase with water. As she placed the flowers in the glass container, Jim's arms wound around her from behind. He smelled of clay, even away from the studio, and the scent and the feel of his warmth against her made her knees go weak.

"How many times can I say I'm sorry?" he whispered, nuzzling her ear then gently kissing the side of her throat.

"No more apologies," she said, tipping her head to give him better access. "I don't want to be beholden to the past." She flipped off the faucet then shivered as his calloused fingers grazed her neck.

"Then let's focus on right now," he said against her skin. "I want you so damn much, Jana. I've barely thought of anything else since you walked out last week."

She turned and he immediately captured her mouth with his, kissing her in exactly the way she liked to be kissed. This moment was different than the one they'd shared in his studio. That had been a shock, nerves skittering through her at how he might judge the woman she'd become, no longer young and beautiful.

But his words and the way he held her—like she was the most precious thing in the world—gave her confidence. As quickly as they'd appeared, her doubts vanished. This felt so right and her heart thundered at the turn her life was taking.

She'd relegated herself to the back burner of her own life, but here she was in the blue center of the flame. She couldn't think of anything she wanted more…except maybe leading Jim Spencer up to her bedroom.

Then she heard the front door open. She yanked

away from his embrace, knocking over the flowers with one nervous hand. The vase clattered to the porcelain but didn't break, and she quickly righted it, refusing to glance at Jim, who'd thankfully taken a few steps to the edge of the island.

"Mom?" Griffin's voice rang out from the entry.

"In the kitchen," she called.

The patter of small feet sounded in the hall a moment before Joey ran around the corner into the room. "We got a tree," he shouted, more animated than she'd seen him since he arrived in Stonecreek. "I named him Freddie. Come and see. Come and see."

His cheeks were flushed, his little arms waving in the air as a huge grin lit his face. Jana's heart lifted at this glimpse of a happy, carefree child unencumbered by the tragedy he'd endured.

"Who are you?" he asked Jim, skidding to a stop in his stocking feet.

"My name's Jim."

"Mr. Spencer is Maggie's dad." Griffin entered the room, darting a vaguely suspicious gaze between Jana and Jim, as if he knew what they'd been doing moments ago.

Jana felt her face go hot and spun away from her son, busying herself with righting the flowers.

"We got Maggie a tree too," Joey told him, unaware of the underlying tension that suddenly filled the room. "Its name is Fiona."

"What a clever idea," Jana said, trying to keep her voice steady, "to name the trees."

"Wait until you see them," Griffin said. "Are we interrupting something? Where'd you get the flowers, Mom?"

"Jim brought them." Jana took a breath and turned, raising a brow at her son to let him know she was not open for commentary on the gift. "We're about to head out to visit the foundry that casts his sculptures."

"I want to give your mom an idea of the process as we're working on a final design for the Harvest commission."

Griffin walked to the refrigerator and grabbed a bottle of water. "I bet that's not all he wants to give you," he said, low enough that only Jana could hear.

So much for quelling him with an arched brow.

"Enough," she whispered then placed the vase of flowers on the island. "I'd like to see your tree," she said to Joey, reaching out to wipe a speck of chocolate from his cheek. "Looks like you stopped at the bakery on your way home."

"Maggie and I got extra whipped cream on our hot chocolate," the boy reported.

"She likes whipped cream." Tenderness was clear in Jim's voice. His eyes clouded as he glanced at Griffin. "I didn't realize the two of you were spending time together again."

Griffin lifted the water bottle to his lips, his movements casual. Still, Jana could almost feel him bristling at the subtle accusation in Jim's tone. "Is that a problem?"

Jim straightened his shoulders, transforming from eclectic artist and ardent kisser to overprotective father in an instant. Even with his defensive stance directed at her son, Jana respected him for it. "I don't want to see her hurt."

A muscle jumped in Griffin's jaw, the same way

it had in his father's when Dave was frustrated or angry. But her son only nodded. "I understand." He set the water bottle on the counter. "I promise I won't hurt her again. She means the world to me."

She held her breath as Jim mulled over the declaration. To say Griffin kept his emotions close to the vest was an understatement, so she knew it had taken a lot for him to reveal any bit of his feelings for Maggie.

"See that you don't," he answered finally. Griffin let out a long breath and nodded.

"Freddie is waiting." Joey tugged on Jana's hand.

She smiled at Jim. "Would you like to meet Freddie?"

"Absolutely," he answered and she felt a deep sense of contentment that all the pieces of her life were finally beginning to fit together.

The more time Griffin spent with Christian Milken, the deeper his distaste for the slick CEO became. He'd given him a tour of the bottling operation today, reviewing the environmental practices they employed, including alternative energy and an extensive recycling program. Some of the details weren't applicable to the technology LiveSoft created but much of the construction initiatives could become a blueprint for how the company built their new headquarters.

"You've been doing this your whole life?" Christian asked, taking in the view of the fields from Griffin's new office. It was actually Trevor's old office. Griffin had expected to feel odd in the space. Instead, it gave him a sense of connection with his brother.

Trevor had been traveling back and forth between Stonecreek and Sonoma, and seemed happier than Griffin had ever seen him. He was already talking about a partnership between Calico and Harvest, and it came as a huge shock to both of them that they were excited to work together.

"No," he admitted without reservation. "I left Stonecreek when I was eighteen to join the army. Did three tours then retired from active duty and worked in the construction industry around the region. I returned to Harvest about six months ago."

Christian looked surprised. "You certainly sound like an expert."

"I've kept tabs on the industry and Marcus has been a great teacher since I've been back."

"You think after all you've seen that you can be happy in this tiny part of the world?"

"Without a doubt. Stonecreek is home."

"It's so damn small."

"So is Timmins."

Christian laughed softly. "True enough. I'm not trying to compare the two. They're equally provincial in my mind."

"Are you having reservations about making a choice for the headquarters?"

"Where we have our headquarters is a part of the branding for the company. LiveSoft is all about helping people to slow down and smell the roses. Our employees are like little cult members with all the meditation and mindfulness. So being in a small town makes sense for growing the business and for the corporate culture."

"Why does it sound like the CEO isn't buying into the branding?"

"Dude, you've got to understand. You're here now, but you chose to come back. Look at your brother moving off to greener pastures. I love my life in Los Angeles. There are things to do and people to see twenty-four/seven."

Griffin wasn't sure what he found more annoying—this grown man using the word *dude* or the fact that the company's leader didn't believe in what his product represented.

Christian didn't seem to notice that Griffin wasn't captivated by his musings on the good life in LA. "I can hop a plane and be in Vegas in an hour or Cabo in just a little longer. Up here is a different world. It's like real life."

"Isn't that the point?" Griffin didn't bother to hide his irritation, and Christian blinked like it shocked him that someone didn't agree with his opinion.

"I'm not knocking it…exactly. We all have to settle down at some point. You know I started LiveSoft as a lark, right? My roommate at Harvard was brilliant—makes Zuckerberg look like a slacker. But he wasn't driven, not the way you need to be to make it these days. He ended up dropping out after the first year, went to Costa Rica to run a tree farm or something. I flew down for spring break junior year and he already had a beta version of the app. It was his brainchild, but I saw the potential in it."

"So you partnered with him?"

Christian was still looking out the window so Griffin clicked on his email, not really caring about the genesis of LiveSoft.

"Hell, no." Christian laughed. "I took it from him."

Griffin's fingers stilled on the mouse and he stood. "Took as in stole?"

Christian held up his hands. "Intellectual property rights are tricky to enforce. He had the idea and the software to support it. I traded him shares in the tree farm for rights to bring LiveSoft to market. Grant was happy as a clam until hurricane season last year. His whole property was wiped out. Poor schmuck." He moved toward the desk and lowered his voice. "But do you know what the best part is?"

"No idea."

"As part of the app, users input a ton of vital statistics. It's more than just shopping habits. They enter workouts, grocery lists, sleep cycles, vacation plans and career goals. I know what cars they drive and the value of their homes. It's all in one place, managed by my company. No one bats an eye, and marketing firms pay huge money for that intel."

"Are you allowed to sell it? I thought part of the draw of the app was confidentiality. My brother said he tried to work with you, but there are so many hoops and nondisclosures to be a designated partner."

"That's true." Christian nodded, and Griffin wanted to wipe the self-satisfied look off his face. "Subscribers pay money because they think we're protecting them. Marketing firms pay money to get access to our lists. I'm selling data on the back end. It's a revenue cash cow all the way around."

"What happens when your customers realize it?"

"Dude. Not going to happen."

"You think you can keep something like that secret?"

"I pay my tech guys very well for that secret."

Griffin felt his stomach tighten at the thought that his town was getting mixed up with such a crook. Yes, LiveSoft was on top now but what would happen when its shady practices were exposed? He didn't care how much Christian paid anyone, there was no keeping secrets in this day and age.

"It's your business." Griffin tried not to let his disgust show on his face. "I guess." Maggie wanted to woo this fraudulent jerk and Griffin wanted to support her no matter what. He only wished there was a way to entice the company but leave its CEO far behind.

"Yeah, and the board only cares that I'm making money for them. We're talking about taking the company public once the location for the headquarters is selected. It's going to make me a very rich man."

"Sounds like you could be based in Stonecreek but travel wherever and whenever you want. Best of both worlds."

"That's a good point." Christian nodded. "It could work out fine, especially if I have someone like Maggie Spencer on my arm."

Griffin stepped around his desk. "I don't think so."

"Seriously?" Christian scoffed. "Come on, dude. That woman is hot for me. She's giving off so many signals she's more overworked than a traffic light in NYC."

"It's Maggie's job to make sure you're happy," Griffin said through clenched teeth. "She wants to win the competition. You might not care for small-town life, but LiveSoft is an exceptional opportunity for Stonecreek. It matters and, therefore, you matter."

"Nah. She likes me. Trust me. I can read women."

"What a talent."

"I heard she used to be engaged to your brother?"

Another subject Griffin had no intention of discussing with this man. "Yes."

"Do you think he could give me any tips on how to get in her pants? I thought I was close the other night, but she got cold feet."

I'm going to kill him, Griffin thought. "Trevor and Maggie have been friends for years," he answered instead. "Just because the wedding didn't work out doesn't mean he'll help you take advantage of her."

"Whoa, there. No one's taking advantage. Let's just say…" Christian winked. "A merger between myself and the lovely Ms. Spencer would be mutually beneficial."

"Right."

"You want to go get a drink?"

"Not tonight." Or ever in a million years, he added silently.

"Too bad. Maggie and I are meeting at O'Malley's. Maybe we'll grab dinner after and…" He wiggled his eyebrows. "Who knows where the night will lead."

Wait. What?

"You have a date with Maggie?" he asked and something must have leaked into his tone because Christian frowned.

"Is that a problem?"

Hell, yeah. A big one.

"Nope. But I'm going to take you up on that drink after all. If you don't mind a third wheel?"

"No worries, dude. Just be sure to make yourself

scarce once she gets a little tipsy. If you know what I mean?"

He was pretty sure Christian meant he had plans to get Maggie drunk and take advantage of her. No way in hell would Griffin let that happen.

He still couldn't understand why Maggie was going out with Christian after the night they'd had together. He hadn't told her he loved her but he'd *made* love to her. She had to understand what that meant. Or did she?

Chapter Eleven

Maggie walked into O'Malley's that night, immediately greeted by Chuck and several regulars.

"Your guys are in the back," Chuck told her.

Her tongue suddenly felt too big for her mouth. "My g-guys?" she stammered.

"It doesn't seem fair." Jenna Phillips, one of the bar's longtime waitresses and Maggie's former babysitter from when she was a girl, bumped her hip like they were dancing. "I've been divorced for five years and can barely scrounge up a date on Match and you've got two hot men vying for your attention."

Maggie shook her head. "No one is vying for me."

Jenna laughed, low and husky from decades of Marlboros. "When was the last time you checked the LiveSoft competition page? I wouldn't have guessed you'd become the Stonecreek Siren, but I guess it fits.

Griffin looked like he wanted to strangle that slick CEO when they walked in earlier."

"What is a Stonecreek Siren?" Maggie asked, her head beginning to swim.

"*Who*, you mean," Chuck clarified. "It's you, darlin'. At least according to the comments on social media."

Maggie hadn't actually viewed any of the latest photos or videos uploaded to the LiveSoft site. Work had been crazy and she'd been too busy at night with her renovation project. She also had to admit that she didn't relish the idea of watching herself take center stage. She'd asked Morgan to view it and make sure she hadn't come out looking like a total fool. Her sister reported back that everything was great, but now Maggie realized the teenager probably hadn't even bothered to look.

Great. She was the Stonecreek Siren.

"It's putting us way ahead on likes and follows," Brett Russell, one of Stonecreek's police deputies— off-duty now—reported. "I set it up to get notifications. If we win, we're hoping some of that increased tax revenue will head in the department's direction." He pulled his phone out of his jacket pocket. "We're up to—"

"Don't tell me," Maggie blurted, holding up a hand. "I'm nervous enough already."

"Public voting is only one part of the equation," Chuck said from behind the bar, as if she didn't realize that already. "The board and senior management team have to review our proposal. I assume you did a good job on it?"

Jenna, Brett and the rest of the bar patrons waited for her answer with intense stares.

She laughed at the thought of being put on the spot by the happy-hour crowd, but nodded at Chuck. "I did my best."

No one looked particularly convinced that her best would be good enough, but then Jenna winked. "Did you bring the cameras tonight? Might be some fireworks."

"The cameras aren't mine," Maggie told them, as if they didn't know that already. "Christian is here to meet with the town council and spend some time at Harvest, but they won't film again until Christmas Eve."

"What did you get him for Christmas?" Brett asked.

Maggie rolled her eyes. "I haven't had time to do any shopping, but Christian isn't on my gift list. He's a business colleague."

"You went on a date with him," Jenna pointed out, none too helpfully as far as Maggie was concerned.

"It was a dinner with his assistant filming the whole time. I didn't want them to use the footage of Jessica in the pageant. I'm guessing you already know that."

"Yeah." Jenna shrugged. "But it doesn't go with the Stonecreek Siren bit quite as well."

Maggie blew out a frustrated breath. "Chuck, can I get a glass of pinot grigio?"

The bartender nodded. "On the house, Ms. Mayor. I'm already counting on being the favorite watering hole for the LiveSoft crowd."

"No pressure," Maggie muttered under her breath but gave the burly bar owner a thumbs-up.

He poured a glass of Harvest Pinot Grigio, and Jenna handed it to her.

Maggie walked toward the game room at the back of the bar. Christian and Griffin stood on the far side, facing a dartboard that hung on the back wall. Both of them turned as she came around the corner, and a group of men playing pool at a nearby table waved a greeting.

"Hey," Christian called. "You want to play the winner?"

She shook her head. "I'm not much for darts."

"Come on," he coaxed as she moved closer. "I'll give you some pointers." He wrapped an arm around her waist and pulled her close. She smiled but shifted away, flicking a gaze at the other patrons and then to Griffin, who was watching her with steely eyes.

"I didn't expect to see you here," she said to him.

"I bet."

Anger and frustration warred in his tone. She wished she could explain that she'd agreed to meet Christian tonight to tell him there could be nothing between the two of them other than friendship. Surely Griffin didn't think she was interested in the other man after what they'd shared. But she couldn't cut Christian out of her life in the middle of the competition for his company.

Maggie took a long swallow of wine before smiling again. "Who's winning?"

"Me, of course," Christian said and she saw Griffin roll his eyes behind the other man's back. "I thought he was going to take me, but he whiffed the last shot."

"He outplayed me," Griffin said, deadpan, and Maggie realized he was doing all this for her. The knowledge did funny things to her heart. It couldn't be easy for a man like Griffin to humor a guy he clearly couldn't stand—schmoozing and glad-handing were skills more aligned with Trevor's wheelhouse. But he was making the effort because LiveSoft, and therefore its CEO, were important to Maggie.

"Your Christmas tree looks great," she said quietly, willing him to understand that this evening wasn't at all what it appeared from the outside. He'd texted a photo of Joey in front of the scraggly tree, a huge smile on his face and the tree covered in ornaments and colored lights.

"Thanks."

"I need another beer," Christian announced, oblivious to the tension sparking around him.

"Jenna should be making her rounds in a few minutes," Maggie offered.

"I'll go the bar," Griffin said tightly.

"That's my bro." Christian took out his wallet. "You need me to spot you some cash?"

Griffin shook his head. "This round's on me. Maggie?"

"I'm good," she said, lifting her half-full glass.

"Indeed you are." Christian chuckled, the only one of them amused by the innuendo.

Maggie watched Griffin walk away, wondering why she hadn't thought to tell him about her plans with Christian earlier. It had seemed inconsequential at the time, but now it felt foolish.

She took a fortifying breath, tamping down her

guilt about the expectations of people in the community and stepped toward Christian. "We need to talk."

"That sounds ominous," he said with a wide grin. "You sure you don't want to play a round of darts? I can help with your form." He reached for her, but she stepped back, placing her wineglass on a nearby high-top table.

"This isn't a date," she blurted. "We aren't dating."

His brows drew together. "It feels like a date to me."

"No. This situation is new for both of us. The competition complicates things. I like you, Christian." That wasn't exactly a lie. He was smart and charming and easy to talk to. Before he'd made it clear he wanted more from her, she'd thought they could be friends. Still, as dedicated as she was to the town, she couldn't sacrifice her own happiness to win a competition. "But I'm not part of the incentive package."

He twirled one of the plastic darts between two fingers. "I thought I made it clear I need a good reason to pick Stonecreek."

"Yes," she agreed slowly. "If you take a look at our proposal, we've given you several. Stonecreek is a great fit for your headquarters. We offer low taxes, minimal regulations, a high-quality talent pool, affordable real estate and low living costs. We'd do everything we can to support the entrepreneurial culture at LiveSoft. I hope to get the chance to welcome you to the town." She pursed her lips then added, "But not to my bed."

"Ouch." He scrubbed a hand over his jaw. "Have you seen what they're calling you online?"

She shook her head. "I just heard about it."

"The folks in Timmins did too. They called about an hour ago with an offer for an additional two million in tax breaks and incentives if LiveSoft comes there."

Maggie felt her eyes widen. Timmins was a similar economic makeup to Stonecreek, although with Mount Hood in their backyard, the town relied more heavily on tourism income. Where would they get the reserves to offer that kind of money?

"That's generous," she whispered.

"I was hoping for generosity of a different sort from you," he said coolly.

"That's funny," a deep voice said from behind Maggie. "Because with talk like that, it sounds like you're hoping to get your teeth knocked in."

Maggie looked over her shoulder to find Griffin glaring at Christian, a beer bottle clenched in each fist.

His gaze locked on hers before returning to the CEO. "You need to apologize to Maggie."

"Dude, chill out." Christian transferred the darts to one hand and reached for a beer with the other.

Griffin placed the two bottles on a table then folded his muscled arms over his chest. "Don't call me dude. This isn't Chris and Grif's excellent adventure."

"No doubt," Christian muttered. "Talk about a buzzkill night."

"I think you're done here," Griffin said, his voice ominously quiet.

"Stonecreek Siren?" Christian bit off an angry laugh. She noticed that his eyes looked glassy and wondered how many drinks he'd had tonight. This man was so different than the charismatic company leader she'd met at the beginning of the month. "More like the Stonecreek Tease. I'm disappointed, Maggie. I thought you cared about your town."

"I do," she whispered, glancing around to realize they were beginning to attract the attention of other patrons. Attention Maggie didn't want or need right now.

"Prove it."

"We're trying." She moved toward him so that they hopefully wouldn't be overheard, tucking her hair behind her ears. "If you think about the people you've met in town and the welcome you've received. Please spend some time reviewing our proposal. I'm sure you'll—"

"I'm not talking about the town." He leaned in, so close she could smell the alcohol on his breath, something strong and acrid. Not just a few beers at happy hour. "I mean *you* prove it. I'm going to walk out of this bar right now. My room number is four twenty-three. I'll expect you there in—"

The sound of her open palm smacking his cheek startled her. She gasped as Christian reeled back with a curse. Holding a hand to his face, he lunged forward only to be stopped by Griffin's hand on his chest.

Maggie was jostled into a table, the force knocking over her wineglass.

"Get the hell out," Griffin growled, his voice like granite.

"Come on, dude. I'm playing. If she wasn't so uptight then—"

Griffin closed his fist on Christian's shirtfront, wrinkling the expensive fabric. "Out of respect for what your company means to this town, you have thirty seconds to clear out of O'Malley's. After that, I'm going to escort you out myself. I couldn't give a damn about your tax revenue, and I know for sure this isn't the kind of place that tolerates men who talk to a woman like she's your personal property. I'm sure as hell not going to let you get away with it."

There were a few shouts of agreement from the other side of the game room.

Christian wrenched free from Griffin's grasp and jabbed a finger in Maggie's direction. "Is this how you want it to end?"

"It doesn't have to end," she said, automatically going into damage control mode. She ignored Griffin's snort of derision. "Things got out of hand tonight," she said. "But don't throw out everything that's gone before because of it. We're the right choice for LiveSoft."

She hated the feeling that she was groveling, but what else could she do? She wasn't about to sleep with the CEO to guarantee a win, yet she had to at least try to smooth the waters between them. "Our relationship isn't over."

Christian looked at her and then Griffin as if seeing them with fresh eyes. Understanding dawned and his mouth curled into a sneer. "Think again, sweetheart." He practically spat the words at her before storming past.

The bar was silent other than a classic Bob Seger song playing from the speakers.

Maggie drew in several long breaths then righted the wineglass with trembling fingers.

"Don't worry about that, hon." Jenna was beside her the next moment. "I'll clean it up."

"I'm sorry," Maggie whispered, and she hoped Jenna understood it was for more than the spilled drink.

"It's fine." Jenna's voice soothed some of the ache inside Maggie. "If a rich, powerful guy like that can't find a girlfriend without bribing one, there's got to be something wrong with him." She nudged Maggie's arm with her shoulder. "Like maybe his junk don't work?"

Maggie gave a small laugh. "I don't know about that." She turned, ready to thank Griffin for rescuing her once again, only to find that he'd disappeared.

"He left right after the other one," Jenna told her. "Hopefully not to track him down."

Maggie swallowed and dug in the cross-body purse she wore for her wallet. "I've got to talk to him," she whispered.

"Your drink's on the house," Jenna said. "Or the table more like it. You go after Griffin. Don't let him get away."

With a sharp nod, Maggie walked through the bar, purposely avoiding eye contact with anyone or answering the myriad of comments and questions she received on her way out.

"What happens now?"

"Does this mean Stonecreek lost?"

"Too bad the cameras weren't filming tonight."

The temperature had risen into the low forties earlier today, melting most of last weekend's snow. Right now it dipped closer to thirty degrees, and the cold night air felt good on Maggie's face as she exited the bar.

Quiet enveloped her as the heavy door slammed shut, and she closed her eyes for a moment, trying to calm her racing heart.

"Please tell me you aren't thinking of going to his room."

She turned at the sound of Griffin's voice. He leaned against the brick building on the other side of the bar's entrance.

Her stomach flipped wildly as if she hadn't seen him in months instead of minutes. "You can't be serious."

"The last thing I heard you tell him was 'our relationship isn't over.'" He straightened, running a hand through his hair as he approached her.

"I was talking about the town. You saw me slap him, Griffin. Wasn't that clear enough for you?"

"I don't know what to think anymore. A few days ago I was in your bed and tonight I have to listen to that CEO chump share his plans to get lucky with you after your date. Your *date*, Maggie."

"It wasn't a date. I agreed to meet him to explain that we weren't going to have a relationship. I thought I could make him understand without jeopardizing the town's chances in the competition."

"By going on a date," he muttered.

"It. Wasn't. A. Date."

"You don't know how it killed me to play nice with him."

She laughed despite her mounting frustration. "That was you playing nice?"

"He's not bleeding."

"I'm sorry I didn't talk to you about my plans for tonight," she said softly.

"You don't owe me that," he answered. He moved forward, reached out and cupped her cheeks between his palms. As always, she revelled in the warmth of his touch. The rough feel of his calloused palms sent sparks racing along her spine. Would this electric response to Griffin Stone ever stop? It was part curse and part blessing. She couldn't decide which would weigh out in the end.

"I didn't mean—"

He placed his two thumbs on the seam of her lips. "When Christian told me he was going on a date with you, it ripped at my heart. But I also understand how badly I messed up when I left for Seattle with only a lame text." He shook his head. "I thought I was doing the right thing at the time."

"It's okay."

"I love you, Maggie."

She pulled away, even as the words ricocheted through her heart. "Don't say that."

Griffin's mouth dropped open and she saw pain, raw and unfiltered, in his gaze before the emotional shutter dropped over his eyes. "I thought that's what you wanted."

"I... Yes... No..." She shook her head, wondering how to explain something she barely understood herself. "I've moved on," she lied.

"You haven't." He crowded her, his warmth easily melting the ice she was trying to keep frozen around her heart.

"I don't trust you," she whispered, miserable for both of them.

"You trusted me enough to let me into your bed," he said, his voice a low rasp.

She closed her eyes and shared the truth that would drive the final wedge between them. "But not enough to open my heart again."

"Maggie."

The word was both a plea and a promise.

"You're here now because it's necessary. You have to settle down for Joey. But what if things change?"

"What things?" he demanded, taking a step back like her words were shards of glass stabbing at him.

"I don't know." She threw up her hands. "What if you get sick of the wine business or small-town life in Stonecreek? You could take him anywhere or leave him with your mom while you—"

"I'd never do that."

She knew he wouldn't desert the boy. Unfortunately, she had no such confidence in his devotion to her. She wanted to believe him, but him leaving had damaged something deep inside her. She'd made a decision about the path her life would take and was too scared to change it now.

"I can't, Griffin," she said, letting a finality she didn't feel color her tone.

"What about the other night?"

"It was lovely," she said quietly. "But a mistake."

"A mistake? Good to know how you really feel."

She kept her gaze on the sidewalk. If she looked into his eyes right now she wouldn't be able to let him go.

"Thank you for coming to my defense tonight," she told him. "Even if between the two of us we ruined Stonecreek's chances of becoming the next

LiveSoft headquarters, I appreciate having you on my side."

"I'll always be on your side."

She swallowed back the sob that threatened to escape.

"Goodbye, Griffin."

"Good night, Maggie," he answered and she walked away before he had a chance to notice the tears streaming down her face.

Chapter Twelve

"Did you find out Santa put you on the naughty list?" Marcus asked the following morning.

Griffin lifted the ax high above his head then swung it down hard, the piece of oak splitting with a satisfying crack. "What the hell are you talking about?"

"You're chopping that wood like you have a personal vendetta against it," Marcus said, flexing his gloved hands. "I think your mom could have an actual bonfire every night for the rest of the season and still have a pile of kindling left over."

"It may snow again," Griffin answered. "The temperatures will drop."

"Have you heard of the nifty invention called a furnace?"

Griffin swiped a hand across his brow, rolled his

shoulders against the ache already forming there. "Did you need something, Marcus?"

"My wedding's coming up in a couple of weeks."

"New Year's Eve." Griffin grabbed another log from the pile and set it on the wood block. "It's on my calendar."

"Brenna pointed out to me last night that I don't have a best man. Would you stand up with me?"

Griffin stilled. "Me?"

"Don't sound so shocked," Marcus said with a soft laugh.

"I *am* shocked." Griffin set the ax on the ground and pulled in a deep breath. "I'm honored, but it's not a good idea."

"Why not?"

Heartache clogged Griffin's throat, making it difficult to get the words out. He walked away a few paces and rearranged several logs on the woodpile as Marcus waited for an answer. Griffin had always admired the other man's seemingly endless patience. He wished he had more of it.

"Is Maggie going to be Brenna's maid of honor?" he asked finally, turning back.

"Of course."

"There's your reason."

"I thought the two of you were working things out."

"Yeah, well…" Griffin massaged a hand along the back of his neck. "I thought so, too, but—"

"You can't give up on her."

Both men turned as Brenna walked up the hill toward them. Griffin glanced at his friend, jealousy winging through him at the obvious love that filled

Marcus's dark eyes. He immediately walked forward and wrapped an arm around Brenna's shoulder, the action at once protective and tender, like he couldn't resist his need to touch the woman he loved. The gaping hole in Griffin's chest widened at the thought that he'd lost his chance for that with Maggie.

"It's hard to give up something that was never really mine," he said without emotion.

"I thought you'd changed when you came back. I thought you were going to fight for Maggie." She stepped away from her fiancé's embrace and toward Griffin. "What about the video?"

Griffin shook his head. "What video?"

"The one Ray Sharpe took at the bar last night." She placed her hands on her narrow hips, one foot tapping like she was dealing with a recalcitrant schoolboy. "Christian Milken is a slimeball."

"No argument here." Griffin shrugged. "But what does that have to do with me giving up on Maggie? I told her I loved her, Brenna. She walked away this time."

"She's scared. You hurt her."

"I know, but I can't make her give me another chance. She might be right that I don't deserve one."

"Coward," Brenna whispered then pulled her phone from her coat pocket. "Press Play." She shoved the phone in front of him, and Marcus came to stand next to Griffin as he hit the play button. The same anger he'd felt last night bubbled to the surface as he watched the events in the bar, this time as an observer. It was difficult to hear all of what was being said until the bar gradually went quiet, but the outrage and disappointment in Maggie's eyes were clear. And the murder in his own.

He got to the point where he stepped in front of her to confront the dirtbag CEO and his breath caught in his throat. During the interchange, Maggie's gaze stayed on him, filled with gratitude and…love. All the emotions she tried to keep hidden from him were clear. She looked beautiful and vulnerable and strong as hell all at the same time, an intoxicating combination.

The realization struck that since he'd returned to Stonecreek six months ago, Maggie had continually put herself on the line to show him how much he meant to her. He'd had nothing to lose, the black sheep of the family coming back home with no plan to stay. He'd made no promises or commitments and given her very little reason to believe he had anything to offer.

She hadn't cared. She'd brought a light to his life, helping him to make peace with his past while giving him hope for the future for the first time in ages. She'd grounded him with her love. For that, he owed her more than he could ever repay.

He couldn't imagine his life without her. He'd promised himself that he wouldn't give up, but Brenna was right. He was a coward. Maggie hadn't fallen easily back into his arms, and he hadn't rolled up his sleeves to fight for her.

She deserved a man who would stay no matter what. She'd let him back into her life after he'd hurt her. No wonder she didn't trust him. He still needed to earn that trust.

He muttered a string of curses then handed the phone to Brenna, shocked to find her grinning at him.

"Sorry," he whispered. "I need to watch my language."

"The language doesn't bother me," she said. "It sounds like you're finally ready to pull your stupid head out—"

"I think you made your point, hon," Marcus said, shaking his head.

"Right." Brenna pocketed the phone then lifted a challenging brow at Griffin. "So what are you going to do about it?"

"I just came to the realization I'm an idiot. Give me a minute to figure out how to make things better." His mind raced as he thought about the possibility of winning her back. It was a challenge he'd find a way to overcome, no matter what.

Jana took the glass of wine Jim handed her and downed half of it in one gulp.

"Nervous?" he asked, a smile curving his lips.

"Are you sure it's okay for me to be here?"

He nodded. "Morgan and Ben went to a basketball game at the high school. They won't be back for hours." He traced a rough finger down her cheek. "Even if they were at home, it would be fine for you to be here too. You're important to—"

"You shared this house with your wife," she blurted, setting down the wineglass on the kitchen table and walking to the window. She lifted her hand to the cold glass, looking out to the cheerfully decorated houses up and down the street. Christmas lights twinkled in the darkness, making the neighborhood look even more charming.

"Yes," Jim agreed slowly. "We were happy here. Just like you and Dave made a life at Harvest. But that has nothing to do with now, Jana. Are you going to let the past ruin this chance we have for a future?"

"I don't want to, but I can't seem to let go." She turned, laughing softly. "No wonder Griffin can't move on from everything he went through with his dad. He has a terrible role model in me. I don't know how to get over having my heart broken over thirty years ago."

"You got over it," he said softly. "You created an amazing life for yourself."

"You make me happy," she told him then added, "and I feel guilty because of it." She clenched her hands until her nails dug into the soft flesh at the centers of her palms. "Because it was always you, Jim. I knew it, and Dave knew it. I loved him, but my heart wasn't whole so I could only ever give him half of it. How can I think I deserve to be happy after that?"

"Jana." He moved closer, laced his fingers with hers. "Of course you deserve happiness. Dave would want it for you just like Charlotte would for me."

"I don't know," she whispered.

"Then let me be sure for both of us," he told her, and warmth infused her heart. "I wasn't able to when we were younger, but I'm different now. You fell in love with a boy, but I want to love you the way a man should. The way you deserve to be loved."

She blinked away the tears that sprang to her eyes. Could this truly be happening? Her heart felt so full it was almost bursting. She leaned up on tiptoes to kiss him.

He deepened the kiss and she happily opened for him, their tongues dancing as liquid heat pooled low in her belly.

"Dad?"

At the sound of Maggie's shocked voice, Jana tried to yank away. How had they not heard her come into the kitchen?

But Jim held tight to her, tucking her against his side.

"Hey, Mags," he said, his voice just the slightest bit breathless. "I didn't expect you to stop by tonight."

"Ya think? I left a few sweaters in the closet upstairs. I guess I should have called first."

Jana finally glanced up from the floor. "We didn't hear you," she mumbled, feeling like a teenager who'd been caught making out by a disapproving parent.

"Are you two…?" Maggie shook her head. "How long…?"

"It's new," Jana said quickly. "If you're not comfortable then—"

"We hope you'll get used to it," Jim interrupted. "Griffin isn't the only guy around here who let a good one slip away. I'm not going to make the mistake again."

Maggie stared for another long moment then gave a soft laugh. "My dad is straightening out his life before me. I don't know whether to feel hopeful or more depressed."

"I vote hopeful," Jim answered. "I've had way more time to figure things out."

Jana lifted on her tiptoes to kiss his cheek then moved out of his embrace and toward Maggie. "You aren't messed up, Maggie. To me it seems like you're doing everything right. I haven't seen so much excitement in this sleepy town in years. You're putting us on the map."

"Not for long," she said, and the remorse that flashed in her eyes made Jana's heart hurt. "I think I ruined our chances of winning the competition."

Jana shook her head. "That's impossible. We've all seen how hard you've worked. Stonecreek has never looked so good."

"I slapped Christian Milken at O'Malley's last night," Maggie said dully. "Everyone in the bar saw and he was really upset."

"What did he do?" Jim asked.

Maggie flashed a watery smile, as if grateful her father assumed the CEO had done something to deserve her ire.

"He made it clear I needed to be willing to offer more than a 'proposal' on the town's strengths in order to win his favor."

"I'll kill him," Jim muttered.

"Griffin had the same response. He stepped in when Christian got angry."

Jana swallowed. She could only imagine her son's reaction to Maggie being threatened. "Did he...?"

"They exchanged words," Maggie told her. "No more. But I can't help thinking I could have handled things better. I was friendly with Christian from the start. Maybe too friendly."

"No." Jana took her hand. "Don't you dare blame

yourself for anything that man did or made you feel. You don't owe him anything."

"It's not what I owe him that has me the most upset," Maggie said miserably. "It's what my actions are going to mean for the town."

"Sweetie, no." Jana glanced at Jim, who looked like he was ready to track down the LiveSoft CEO and challenge him to an old-fashioned duel for besmirching his daughter's honor. But Jana knew that wasn't what Maggie needed at the moment. It dawned on her that she could have a place in this house and in this family's life. Despite everything that had gone before, the pain Jim had caused her and the decades of animosity between the Stones and Spencers, she cared about all of them.

She couldn't begrudge Jim the life he'd shared with Charlotte. Yes, he'd hurt her but she'd gone on to find a unique happiness with Dave. She'd raised two amazing sons and now ran a successful business. She had no regrets because there was no way she'd give up any piece of the life she built.

Now she had a second chance with her first love. He'd been through plenty yet was still willing to risk loving her again. For this to work, they'd have to find a way to support the other's children even if they were at odds.

How would her boys have turned out without her? Jana could barely force herself to consider the idea. Maggie lost her mother at fifteen, a difficult age for any girl. She was an amazing woman, and Jana wouldn't let anyone make her feel differently.

"I've seen a lot in my years in this town," she said gently. "No one should expect you to compromise your values or allow yourself to be treated like a commodity."

Maggie bit down on her lower lip. "I hope you're right. I thought I could make it better, smooth things over with Christian without jeopardizing our chances. Instead, I made him angry and I pushed Griffin away in the process."

"Griffin cares about you," Jana said without hesitation.

"He told me he loved me," Maggie said with a sniff. "Again."

"He has a funny way of showing it," Jim muttered and Jana didn't even take offense. She understood how badly her son had hurt Maggie. She'd once felt the same kind of heartbreak.

"Are you going to give him another chance?" she asked, squeezing Maggie's hand.

Maggie shook her head. "I told him I couldn't. I can't risk being hurt like I was before."

"Sometimes…" Jana looked toward Jim then back at Maggie "…you have to risk the hurt to find the happiness."

"Sometimes," Maggie responded, "the risk is too great." She swiped at her cheeks then smiled. "I'm happy for the two of you. Really. It's going to make for some strange family get-togethers, although at this point strange feels like our new normal."

"I love you, Mags," Jim whispered and pulled his daughter in for a tight hug. "You deserve so much happiness."

"I'll find it eventually," she answered but Jana could still see the pain enveloping her. "I'm going to grab the clothes and take off."

"You don't need to go," Jana said quickly. "If you want to spend time with your dad—"

Maggie held up a hand. "You two crazy kids continue with…" She waved a hand. "Well, I don't want to know how you're going to continue. But I would like to be a fly on the wall when you explain this to Grammy."

Jana grimaced and Jim let out a laugh. "Your grandmother will just have to deal."

"Yeah," Maggie agreed with a wink. "Good luck with that."

She turned and walked out of the kitchen. Jana slapped her palm to her forehead. "I'm a middle-aged woman, and I'm terrified that your mother won't approve of me. That's sad."

"She'll approve," Jim assured her, wrapping his arms around her once again. "Mom respects you, and for good reason. You're amazing, Jana. The fact that you can comfort Maggie when she tells you she won't give your son another chance is a testament to your character."

"They're adults." She sighed. "I'm certainly not in a position to judge anyone for the choices they make. I love my son, and I think he truly loves Maggie. I still have hope." She rested her head against his chest, taking solace in the steady beat of his heart. "I'm not giving up on them getting another chance at happiness."

"Thank you," he whispered, kissing the top of her head, "for giving me one." He pulled back, cradling her face in his big hand. "Is it too soon for me to tell you I love you?"

Her heart seemed to skip a beat; an avalanche of

joy tumbled through her. "It's not too soon." The truth was she'd never stopped loving this man. She'd buried the emotion to survive without him. But now love that had lain dormant all these years unfolded inside her like the first bloom of the spring pushing through the dry winter earth.

"I love you, Jana." He kissed her, and she breathed him in, feeling more alive than she had in years.

"I love you too," she whispered. "I always will."

Chapter Thirteen

Griffin looked up from the computer as the door to the home office opened and his mother stepped into the room.

"You're up late," his mom said, inclining her head. "Still trying to get up to speed before Marcus leaves?"

"Not exactly." He glanced at the clock on his computer screen then back at her. "You had a late night, as well. Book club gone wild?"

She smiled and shook her head. "I was with Jim Spencer."

Griffin tried to hide his frown but by the look on his mom's face, he didn't succeed. "How long does it take to design a sculpture? I thought you were going with some kind of homage to the seasons."

"Jim and I are together," she said by way of an answer. "I'm in love with him, Griffin."

Talk about an unexpected punch to the gut. "How is that possible? You barely…" Realization dawned like a painfully bright sunrise after an all-nighter. "He's the guy you dated before Dad?"

She nodded and smoothed a hand over her dark sweater. "It didn't help your father to feel any friendlier toward the Spencers over the years."

"Because Jim hurt you." Griffin pushed back from the desk, folding his arms over his chest. "Dad probably wanted to rip him to pieces."

"We never discussed it," she answered. "But that was a long time ago."

"Who cares how long it's been, Mom? He treated you badly. How can you say you're in love with him now?"

"I'm not sure I ever fell out of love," she admitted. "Which doesn't change or diminish what your father and I had." She held up a hand when Griffin would have argued. "I don't owe you an explanation for the workings of my heart. I love you to pieces and would do anything for you, Griffin. For either you or Trevor, and now Joey too. But this decision belongs to me."

"Jim *hurt* you," he repeated, still remembering the sorrow that had filled his mother's gaze when she'd talked about her past.

"You hurt Maggie," she countered.

He sucked in a breath. Jana Stone with a swift uppercut that left him reeling.

"It's not the same thing."

"Are you sure?"

"No," he admitted, swallowing hard. "At this point, I'm not sure of anything except that I love her and I've lost her."

"Oh, Griffin."

He flicked a hand toward the computer screen. "I'm looking into Christian Milken's history now. The guy seems like the all-American corporate captain of technology, but he's shady."

"Maggie told us about her run-in with him." His mother stepped forward. "And yours."

"You would have been proud." He flashed a quick smile. "I didn't kill him."

"I'm proud of you for so many reasons."

"Brenna called me a coward for not fighting harder to win Maggie back."

"I've always liked that girl."

"I bet." He chuckled. "I don't want to give up on her."

"Then don't."

He rested his elbows on the desk, placing his head in his hands. "I'm so damn scared of failing."

His mother's sharp intake of breath reverberated in the quiet of the room. Griffin didn't look up. He wouldn't be able to say the things he needed to share if he had to meet her gaze.

"I tried with Dad. Not in the way he wanted, but I tried. And no matter what I did, it was never enough. I learned everything I could about the vineyard. I made his passion my passion, and he still wouldn't let me in. At some point, it became easier to disappoint him. If I made that my goal, at least I could succeed at something. I was never enough for him, and part of me thinks I'll never be enough for Maggie."

"You're enough," his mother whispered, her voice filled with tears.

"You have to say that. You're my mom." He was

trying to make a joke because the emotions pouring through him made him anxious, itchy like a junkie craving the needle.

"Maggie loves you," she said, her tone grave. So much for lightening the mood. His heart threatened to beat out of his chest in response to her words.

"Look at what I did to her," he said after several long moments. "I'm worried about you with her father because he hurt you in the same way I hurt Maggie. I wish it could be different."

"You're living in the past," she said. "I know because I spent decades there. But you and Maggie still have a chance, Griffin. It's only too late if you believe it."

"I need to show her I'm worth the risk."

"Then show her."

"Will you help me?"

"Whatever you need." His mom grabbed a ladder-back chair that sat against the wall and pulled it toward the desk. "Do you know the last time you asked me for help was on your fourth-grade science project?"

He laughed for real this time. "I was an idiot even as a kid."

"You're just a slow learner," she said, ruffling his hair like she used to when he was a boy.

"I can't live without her," he whispered and took comfort in his mother's knowing smile.

"I have a feeling you won't have to."

Maggie approached the town square on Christmas Eve with a heavy heart. She knew the video of her slapping Christian had made the rounds through the community, although no one but Brenna had actually mentioned it to her.

It was never a good sign when the town went radio silent. She didn't have the nerve to address it herself, hoping beyond hope the damage hadn't been as bad as she thought.

No one from Christian's team had returned her calls, although she'd gotten a terse text from Allyson that he would honor his commitment to attend the town's annual Christmas Eve caroling event. It was scheduled to be the final activity filmed for the competition.

The community always came together en masse for a public reading of "The Night Before Christmas" and a selection of holiday songs led by the high school chamber choir. It had always been one of her family's favorite traditions. Her mom had loved it especially, and Maggie could still remember that final holiday they'd had together. Her mom had been in a wheelchair, with Ben cradled in her lap. Tears streamed down her face as she sang in her lilting soprano about "little Lord Jesus asleep on the hay."

Both Maggie and her father had been in denial, not willing to admit that they wouldn't have another Christmas together. Miracles happened all the time in movies and television shows. Why not in their little corner of the world?

But there had been no reprieve from cancer. Instead, her mother had died on a cold, dreary afternoon in late January. The following Christmas had been bittersweet and her father had withdrawn into himself. But her mom had made Maggie promise that she'd keep up the traditions they loved so much for Morgan and Ben. She'd forced her dad out of the house, and with Grammy's help, they'd bundled up the two little ones and all of them had attended the Christmas Eve event.

It had been a turning point of sorts. Her father had remained steeped in grief, but after that night there were glimmers of hope in the darkness that had engulfed their lives. For Maggie, the festive occasion had taken on special meaning.

Tonight it felt tainted by her anxiety over the situation with LiveSoft. She wasn't sure how to fix the relationship and still be true to herself. Honestly, she wasn't sure if she wanted to. If Christian believed he could use his position to take advantage of her, would he also abuse his influence in the community if his company moved to Stonecreek? Maggie didn't want to give so much potential negativity any hold in her town, but she couldn't deny the impact headquartering such a growing company would have on the community.

"Come on," her brother called from the sidewalk across the street. "We're going to miss the first part. Grammy's saving us a spot up front."

Maggie smiled as she jogged across the empty street toward Ben, Morgan and their father. This year Morgan's boyfriend, Cole, and Jana Stone joined them.

"Let's hurry then," she said when she got closer, looping an arm over Ben's shoulder as they started walking toward the center of the square. "I don't want you to be late." It made her heart glad that even at fourteen, her brother hadn't outgrown attending these types of events.

Even Morgan looked happy to be there, which probably had a lot to do with the tall, nervous-looking boy holding tight to her hand. In the past couple of months, Morgan had finally released her need to rebel, morphing into a friendly, outgoing young woman with a beautiful spirit to match. She'd gotten a job as an after-school babysitter for one of the neighborhood families and spent much of her free time volunteering at the community center.

Maggie's father looked particularly content as well as he stuck close to Jana's side. Maggie didn't dare ask about Griffin and Joey. It was crazy how much she missed both of them even though the decision to break things off had been hers.

Ben wound around the edge of the crowd gathered in front of the stage that had been erected by volunteers early this morning. The night was clear and cold but not unbearably so. The couples and families standing near the front parted to let Maggie and her group through. She could imagine Grammy barking orders about how she was saving the front row.

She sucked in a breath then plastered on a smile as she realized Christian and his loyal assistant were standing next to Vivian. Allyson turned her ever-present phone toward Maggie to record her arrival, and Christian gave her a terse smile.

"Merry Christmas," Maggie said, hugging her grandma.

"Merry Christmas *Eve*," Grammy corrected, as was her way.

"Of course," Maggie agreed then inclined her head

toward Christian. "We hope you enjoy our town's last official event before Christmas."

"Timmins hosted a parade in my honor. I'm not sure how you expect to compete with a story and a few songs."

Maggie opened her mouth to answer, but her father moved to her side, placing a hand on her arm but addressing Christian. "We don't have to compete," he said, his tone flinty. "Tonight you're a guest in our town, and we're proud of our traditions. We don't have to go overboard for the camera. No one here owes you anything, young man." He pointed a finger at Christian. "You'll do well to remember that."

"Oh, snap," Morgan whispered.

With one last glare thrown at Christian, Jim stepped back to stand next to Jana on the far side of Morgan and Cole.

"Delete that part," Christian muttered to Allyson under his breath.

The young woman gave Maggie an almost sympathetic glance then nodded.

At that point, Chuck O'Malley took the stage. "Welcome everyone," he said into the microphone. "It's an exciting evening and we're glad you took the time out of your busy holiday schedule to join us." He adjusted the red Santa cap perched on his head. "The town has hosted this Christmas Eve event for the past seventeen years, and I've had the honor of reading this special poem each Christmas Eve. I'd like to take a moment to thank the late writer Clement Clarke Moore, who first penned the poem titled, 'Account of a Visit from Saint Nicholas.' We know this beloved tale better as 'The Night Before Christ-mas.'" There was a round of applause and Chuck made an exaggerated bow.

Then he pulled a pair of wire-rimmed glasses from his shirt pocket and perched them on his nose. "Without further ado," he said with a win, "let's get started. All of you big and little kiddies out there need to hit the hay on time tonight so Santa Claus can make his rounds." He opened a well-worn book and began to recite the poem.

Maggie had always loved the juxtaposition of the burly bar owner showing a sentimental side with his impassioned recitation of the Christmas classic.

This year was no exception and by the time Chuck got to the last line, everyone joined in on a chorus of "Merry Christmas to all, and to all a good night."

Everyone except Christian, who looked bored out of his mind. The man had somehow morphed into Stonecreek's own personal Grinch. Chuck didn't seem to notice as he wiped at the corner of his eye with the edge of one sleeve. "Gets me every time," he whispered into the microphone. "Before we begin with the caroling portion of the evening, there's someone special I'd like to invite to the stage. This young man is relatively new to our community, but we hope he'll be a part of Stonecreek for many years to come."

Out of the corner of her eye, Maggie saw Chris-tian roll his eyes, clearly not relishing taking any part in the evening. She hated that he was going to take center stage for something so personal to her and that meant so much to the town.

"Please join me in welcoming little Joey Barlow and, with him, Griffin Stone."

Christian took a step forward then froze and quickly backed up again, his mouth twisting into a brittle frown.

Joey walked up the steps to the stage, holding tight to Griffin's hand. Chuck ushered Griffin toward the microphone as he patted the boy's head.

"Hey, everyone," Griffin said with a tight smile.

"Hey, Griffin," the crowded shouted back instantly.

His shoulders relaxed ever so slightly. "It's been a few years since I've attended one of these holiday events," he admitted then grimaced. "In fact, I think the last time I was here for Christmas Eve, I indulged in too much eggnog in the alley behind the bakery."

"It took me a month to get the stink out," Dora shouted from the back of the square.

"Sorry about that," Griffin called with a wave of his hand. "But it's a good segue into why I asked Chuck if Joey and I could borrow the mic for a few minutes." He glanced over his shoulder at the burly bar owner. "Just for this year. I promise."

Chuck nodded.

"When Joey heard about the reading of 'The Night Before Christmas,'" Griffin continued, "he was pretty excited because that was his mommy's favorite Christmas story."

Joey tugged on the hem of Griffin's canvas jacket then lifted his arms to be picked up. When Griffin obliged, Joey whispered into his ear. Griffin hugged the boy then spoke into the microphone. "Joey's come to live in Stonecreek because his mom died this year." An immediate hush fell over the crowd.

"Yes…well…" Griffin cleared his throat. "Since it's his first Christmas here, I wanted him to see what an amazing town we have. I kind of ignored that fact for a lot of years. It's become clear since I've been back that there's no place I'd rather be." He shrugged. "There really is no place like home."

Applause and cheers erupted, and Griffin's gaze slammed into Maggie's. "I'm here for the long haul," he said directly to her, "and you're the reason for it."

Her heart gave a staccato thump in her chest.

"As you might have heard," he told the audience, "Stonecreek has been participating in a bit of a social media frenzy for the past couple of weeks. A competition, you might call it."

More applause but it was less enthusiastic. Allyson held up her camera to take in the crowd behind her.

"I think we can all agree it's been exciting to showcase the best parts of our community so that people can see how special this place is. It's been a good reminder for me, anyway, about what's most important in my life." He glanced toward Maggie again, and there was nothing but love in his beautiful green eyes.

No doubt. No defenses. All love and all aimed at her.

"Damn girl," someone said from the row behind her. "I wish a fine man would look at me that way."

"I love you, Maggie," he said clearly. "I've let a lot of things get in the way of that, especially my own stupidity."

She gave a shuddery laugh and clasped a hand

over her mouth. Never in a million years would she have imagined Griffin professing his love in front of most of the town. Particularly when she'd told him they didn't have a chance. For all he knew, he was putting himself out there for nothing. Risking everything.

"I know I've given you plenty of reasons not to trust me, and I won't blame you at all if you never want to talk to me again after this night." He paused, swallowed then said, "But I will love you forever. I love your passion and your heart and your dedication. I love that you don't let me get away with much. I love that no matter where I am in the world, you will always be my home."

"Oh, my," Grammy whispered next to her. "Oh, my."

Oh, my indeed. Maggie didn't know what to think. Her heart felt like it was going to explode in her chest.

"And here's something else we can all agree on," he said to the crowd in general. "Our mayor, Maggie Spencer, has gone above and beyond in working to make sure Stonecreek is the top contender for the LiveSoft headquarters. She's done everything except—" he held up one finger "—let herself be bullied and harassed by LiveSoft's CEO."

He looked out to the audience. "Is it uploaded, Trevor?"

To Maggie's utter shock, Trevor made his way to the front of the assembled crowd.

"Sure is," he called to Griffin. "With the hashtag 'livesoftnotwrong.'"

"Catchy turn of phrase," Griffin said with a

thumbs-up to his brother. "For those of you who haven't heard, Maggie had an unfortunate incident with Christian Milken a few nights ago where the jerk propositioned her in return for the promise of Stonecreek winning the competition." Griffin held out a hand at the outraged murmurs that snaked through the crowd.

Maggie felt her eyes widen and glanced toward Christian, whose face was turning bright red with anger.

"Now we have someone from LiveSoft filming tonight's event." He focused his gaze on Allyson. "You are still filming, right?"

The woman nodded just as Christian snatched the phone from her hand. "Not very sporting of you, Milken," Griffin said. "But no matter. We've invited a news crew from Portland to attend our Christmas Eve celebration. They've been helpful enough to upload the video taken of Christian harassing our Maggie onto their homepage. So please..." He nodded to the crowd. "Share and retweet and don't forget my brother's clever hashtag." He pointed a finger at Christian. "'Livesoftnotwrong.'"

"This is ridiculous," Christian shouted. "I didn't like this place from the start."

"*You* are ridiculous," Griffin shot back. "Stonecreek is amazing. Maggie is amazing. One of the things that makes this town so special is our community. We aren't going to see anyone disrespected the way you tried to with her. No headquarters is worth compromising our values."

Thunderous applause broke out and Christian stormed past Maggie, Allyson following quickly in his wake. "I'm sorry," the assistant whispered as she passed.

"And now," Griffin said when the applause finally died down. "Let's have our high school choir lead us in a few carols."

Maggie stood stock-still for a few seconds, stunned as friends surrounded her offering words of support and encouragement. As the choir filled the stage, she stepped away from the crowd, trying to catch her breath. What had Griffin done?

"Is this true?" Grammy demanded, making her way to Maggie's side.

"Yes, but…"

"If that man comes near you again," Vivian said, fire in her eyes. "I'll personally shank him."

"Yeah, Grammy," Ben shouted. He and Morgan had followed her, along with their father and Jana.

"I'm sorry about the competition," Maggie whispered to her grandmother. "I tried—"

"No." Grammy shook her head. "Nothing is more important to me than you, Mary Margaret. It doesn't matter what happens in this town as long as my family is safe and happy. You all mean the world to me."

Maggie didn't bother to wipe away the tears that rolled down her cheeks.

"I hate seeing you cry," a familiar voice said from behind her. She turned to where Griffin stood several feet away.

The people around her seemed to fade into the background as she moved toward him until they stood toe-to-toe.

"They're happy tears," she whispered. "That was some speech."

"I meant every word of it." He wiped at her cheeks with the pads of his thumbs, and the familiar fire sparked low in her belly at his touch. Only this time she didn't fight it. "I love you so much, Maggie. I'm sorry I hurt you."

She touched a finger to his lips. "No apologies."

"Then let me—" he wrapped his fingers around hers "—spend the rest of our lives proving that I deserve to be at your side. Give me a chance to make you as happy as you make me."

"I love you," she whispered, and he blew out a breath like those words were a balm to his soul.

To her utter shock, he dropped to one knee and pulled a small black box from his jacket pocket. "I love you, Maggie. I will love you and cherish you forever if you say yes. Will you marry me?"

He opened the box to reveal a beautiful diamond solitaire. Then he crooked a finger and Joey came running over to perch on Griffin's knee. "Will you marry both of us?" Griffin amended and the boy added, "Please?"

"Say yes," someone shouted and she glanced around to realize that the choir had stopped singing and most of the town was watching Griffin propose to her.

"It's our home," he said when her gaze met his again. "I guess it's only fitting that they be a part of this."

"Yes," she said through another round of tears. "Yes, I'll marry you. Yes, I'll give you as many chances as you need. Yes, I'll love you forever."

He slipped the ring onto her finger and then she was in his arms. As she hugged Joey and kissed Griffin, the people she'd known and loved her whole life surrounded them with good wishes. Maggie might not be able to carry a tune, but her heart sang as she finally had everything she'd ever wanted.

Epilogue

"He's dancing." Griffin took Maggie's hand in his and squeezed her fingers. "I can't believe she got him out there."

Maggie smiled as she watched Ellie and Joey twirl to the music amidst the other dancers at Brenna and Marcus's wedding reception. It had been a beautiful ceremony, elegant yet understated with Brenna gorgeous in an off-white sheath dress with a beaded lace overlay. Marcus had seemed almost ready to burst into tears when she'd appeared to walk down the aisle, and Maggie was so happy for her friend. The ceremony had taken place at the small chapel across the street from The Miriam Inn while the reception was being held in the hotel's banquet room.

They'd kept the guest list small, so everyone knew each other. It was turning into a lively celebration of both the marriage and the impending New Year. Maggie smiled in response to the cheeky grin Ellie gave Joey. Although the boy looked more than a little nervous, it was obvious he was having fun with his new best friend.

"How could he say no?" Maggie laughed. "He's smitten."

"I know the feeling," Griffin said, and her heart seemed to skip a beat at the love radiating from his gaze.

"I never imagined I could be this happy," she whispered.

Griffin leaned in and brushed a gentle kiss across her lips. "Just wait until our wedding day."

Tiny shivers of anticipation zipped along her spine. "Do you think we can really get away with inviting only family?"

"We've spent plenty of time in the Stonecreek spotlight recently. We've earned a little privacy."

"At least the national morning shows have stopped calling," she said, cringing slightly.

The fallout from the situation with LiveSoft had been both positive and challenging. The video documenting Christian's treatment of her had gone viral, and he'd been forced to resign from the company. They'd named one of the VPs as acting CEO, but from what Maggie'd heard, the board of directors was trying to woo the man who'd created the original app to come on board with the company.

She couldn't bring herself to feel sorry for Christian. No one should be allowed to abuse their power in that way, and she was proud and grateful that her town had rallied around her.

In the wake of the negative press, LiveSoft had decided to remain headquartered in California for the foreseeable future. But Maggie'd received a call yesterday from a company that manufactured a variety of outdoor-lifestyle products from coolers to apparel. The company had outgrown its original headquarters and was interested in Stonecreek as a possible relocation site. She'd set up a meeting with the owners after the first of the year and felt cautiously optimistic about bringing the business to town.

Either way, she felt confident that Stonecreek would continue to grow and thrive under her leadership. Despite the stress from the LiveSoft competition, she'd learned to believe in herself. Heck, she'd even showered this morning in her brand-new bathroom. Not many people spent Christmas vacation tiling a bathroom, but her family and friends had pitched in to help her finish the job.

"I think we're finally going to return to normal life around here," Griffin told her.

"You won't find normal boring?" she asked, laughing as he tugged her to her feet.

"Life with you could never be boring, Maggie May." He led her to the dance floor, and despite the up-tempo song, wrapped his arms around her waist and slowly swayed to the music.

"Worst dancers ever," Morgan muttered as she shimmied by.

"Come on, Griffin," Cole called as Morgan joined him and Ben on one side of the dance floor. "Let's see that white man's overbite."

Griffin rolled his eyes at the trio. "Maybe later."

"I love your moves," Maggie told him and he held her tighter.

"I love you," he whispered.

She rested her head on his chest and closed her eyes, grateful for everything that had brought her to this moment and to a love she knew would last forever.

* * * * *

SPECIAL EXCERPT FROM

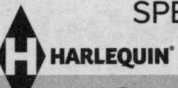 HARLEQUIN®

SPECIAL EDITION

*Arizona park ranger Vivian Hollister is not having
a holiday fling with Sawyer Whitehorse—no matter
how attracted she is to her irresistible new partner.
So why is she starting to feel that Sawyer is the one
to help carry on her family legacy? A man to have
and to hold forever...*

*Read on for a sneak preview of
A Ranger for Christmas,
the next book in the Men of the West miniseries
by USA TODAY bestselling author Stella Bagwell.*

She rose from her seat of slab rock. "We'd probably better
be going. We still have one more hiking trail to cover before
we hit another set of campgrounds."

While she gathered up her partially eaten lunch, Sawyer
left his seat and walked over to the edge of the bluff.

"This is an incredible view," he said. "From this distance,
the saguaros look like green needles stuck in a sandpile."

She looked over to see the strong north wind was hitting
him in the face and molding his uniform against his muscled
body. The sight of his imposing figure etched against the
blue sky and desert valley caused her breath to hang in her
throat.

She walked over to where he stood, then took a cautious
step closer to the ledge in order to peer down at the view
directly below.

"I never get tired of it," she admitted. "There are a few
Native American ruins not far from here. We'll hike by
those before we finish our route."

A hard gust of wind suddenly whipped across the ledge and caused Vivian to sway on her feet. Sawyer swiftly caught her by the arm and pulled her back to his side.

"Careful," he warned. "I wouldn't want you to topple over the edge."

With his hand on her arm and his sturdy body shielding her from the wind, she felt very warm and protected. And for one reckless moment, she wondered how it would feel to slip her arms around his lean waist, to rise up on the tips of her toes and press her mouth to his. Would his lips taste as good as she imagined?

Shaken by the direction of her runaway thoughts, she tried to make light of the moment. "That would be awful," she agreed. "Mort would have to find you another partner."

"Yeah, and she might not be as cute as you."

With a little laugh of disbelief, she stepped away from his side. "Cute? I haven't been called that since I was in high school. I'm beginning to think you're nineteen instead of twenty-nine."

He pulled a playful frown at her. "You prefer your men to be old and somber?"

"I prefer them to keep their minds on their jobs," she said staunchly. "And you are not *my* man."

His laugh was more like a sexy promise.

"Not yet."

Don't miss
A Ranger for Christmas *by Stella Bagwell,*
available December 2018 wherever
Harlequin® *Special Edition books and ebooks are sold.*

www.Harlequin.com

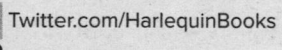

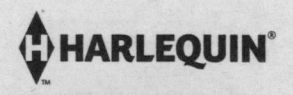